Rutheria

The Plateau

Klymora

Gaia

The Mhuhu

Rioghail

Caledonia

The Cari

Zhongguo

THE PRINCE OF KLYMORA

KINGDOMS AND CURSES
BOOK THREE

Daphne Paige

THE PRINCE OF KLYMORA

Copyright © 2024 by Daphne Paige

Second Edition August 2025

Find the author on Instagram @daphne.paige.books

Cover design by Daphne Paige, images and fonts
licensed through Envato Elements

Chapter designs by Daphne Paige

Editing by Jackie Marie and Brenda Woody

Published by Popcorn Publishing in the United States of
America

Popcorn Publishing

To Barnaby, our inspector.

THE PRINCE OF KLYMORA

KINGDOMS AND CURSES
BOOK THREE

Pronunciation Page

Ayne—(Ann)

Edelweiss—(Eh-dell-wise)

Kaiva—(Kai-vah)

Macellen—(Mah-kell-en)

Faramund—(Fair-ah-mund)

Klymora—(Kly-more-ah)

Gaia—(Guy-ah)

Abhainn—(Ah-bay-n)

Luvenia—(Loo-ven-e-ah)

Tavo—(Tah-vo)

Caz—(Ca-az)

Zhongguo—(Zhong-guo)

CHAPTER ONE

The Assassin

T alin narrows his eyes at the man clad in black. He tightens a rope around the man's wrists, ignoring him as he winces. Talin hopes it hurts. After all Faramund has done, all those whose lives he's affected, he deserves a little pain.

"Faramund, traveler, spy, and assassin. You are under arrest by Prince Talin of Klymora for the murder of King Archibald Macellen. You will be tried in front of the court, and they will decide your fate. Do you have anything to say?" Talin asks, leaning closer to Faramund. He can smell the sweat and grime on the assassin's skin—plastered there from his attempt to escape. After he heard Talin was searching for him, he took off across Klymora— Talin assumes Stella assisted him—but his mother's help was to no avail. Talin caught up to the assassin in Dunbar.

"Talin," Faramund starts, his voice full of regret.

Talin spits at Faramund's feet. His eyes are red with rage. "*Prince* Talin to you. You killed my father and had the nerve to try to be my friend."

Faramund blows out a breath. His keen eyes flick from Talin to the sun-speckled hedges bordering the nearest property. Through grinding teeth, he says, "We *were* close, *Prince* Talin."

Talin scoffs. "Like Scota we were. I never trusted you, Faramund. Apparently for good reason. I should thank Ayne for telling me about you and what you did." He pinches his eyes closed, trying to force away tears. "You took my father from me. Do you know what that did to me? A child shouldn't be forced to grieve, Faramund."

Faramund sighs. His dark eyes land on Talin once again. "I know what it's like to grieve. I know what it's like to be unwanted, Prince Talin. Don't think you're the only one with hardships."

Talin snarls, harshly tugging Faramund back by the ropes tied around his wrists. Faramund stumbles and falls to the muddy ground, and Talin plants his foot on his chest. "My hardships, as you say, were dealt by your hand. You will see justice for your actions. Mark my words. And, if for some Scota-forsaken reason, they let you go, I will hunt you down and kill you the same way you killed my father." Talin gestures for a pair of guards standing beside his carriage to come and collect the weasel. When the guards draw near, he whispers, "If he tries anything, don't hesitate to straighten him out."

The guards nod and drag Faramund to his feet, shoving him toward the first sleek black carriage. Talin watches them for a moment before climbing into the carriage behind the one transporting the criminal.

"Back home, Your Highness?" his coachman asks, readying his grip on the horses' lead.

"Yes. Quick as possible." Talin looks out the window as his coachman shuts the door. He should feel angry, sad, confused even. But he doesn't feel anything. He watches the landscape roll by. His face

3

is empty of emotion. If someone were to look at him right now, they'd think he's bored.

Talin sighs and leans back against the upholstered seat, his eyes lazily roaming over the green hills and tall trees. He glances over at the empty spot beside him, longing to see the bright face of his friend smiling back at him. He wants to take her hand, to smirk at the blush on her cheeks, and to chuckle as her etiquette slips, allowing him to just see *her*. Beautiful Ayne.

He swallows. *Now*, his emotions return. He wonders what Ayne is doing now, all the way in Zhongguo. Maybe she's meeting with the emperor, dining with those of noble blood, sleeping in a bed with sheets far richer than those in Klymora.

His mind returns to the ball he hosted for her and the little white gerbil she had on her shoulder.

Talin will be bored now, returning to his everyday life before Ayne. Sulking in his room. Commanding the court. Laying under the elm tree; *their* elm tree. Listening to the wind whistling by, the shouts down at the dock, and the Abhainn River sloshing below.

A bitter taste floods his mouth, and he frowns. *Life isn't as bright without you, Ayne.*

CHAPTER TWO

The Secret

Talin follows the guards down a flight of stairs and into the musky dungeon beneath the palace. His shoes squish as he steps in a puddle of still water, and he groans, trying to shake the liquid off. He gives up and returns his gaze to Faramund as he's pushed inside the farthest cell. The assassin's dark clothes make him hard to pick out in the shadows. *Good*, Talin thinks, *it's a blessing to not see you.*

He turns around to head back out of the tunnels when Faramund's serpent-like voice finds him, echoing slightly in the small chambers.

"This isn't the end, Prince Talin. You and I both know *that*." He chuckles darkly.

Talin ignores the goosebumps that dot his arms. He rests his hand on the small, elaborate dagger at his waist. "Yes, it is." He leaves as his words are still ringing in the air.

He steps through the doorway from the dungeon and into the sunny corridor, sensing evil lurking nearby. Glancing to the right, his heart picks up pace. He slips behind the open door as his mother nears, her heels clicking on the stone floor. Her aura of darkness and cruelty consumes the space around her. She doesn't notice Talin hiding. She storms down the steps to the dungeon. Talin bites his cheek, taking a deep breath as he peers into the shadows he just left.

Talin's curiosity gets the best of him, so he ducks back through the doorway, hiding in the shadows of the entryway and listening to Stella as she talks to Faramund. He's scared to breathe. His mother reminds him of the dragons he's read about in books when he was younger: all-powerful. She can kill with a single swipe of her claws and doesn't hesitate to take what she wants.

"What are you doing in here, Faramund?" Stella growls. Talin can hear her foot tapping the floor.

"He found me," Faramund replies, his voice dripping with anger.

"Well, *clearly*," Stella retorts. She huffs and Talin imagines her crossing her arms. "How are you going to get out of here?"

"What would be the point? He'd find me again. He's not going to give up, my queen," Faramund exclaims.

Talin sinks to the floor and presses closer to the wall, furrowing his brow. The back of his tunic sticks to his skin with the dampness that leeches from the dungeon wall.

Stella paces before stopping once again. Her voice is hard with determination. "We'll have to take care of him then."

Faramund exhales. "You're sure?"

Stella takes a deep breath and sighs. "I'm sure. If he's going to stand in our way, Faramund, then he has to go."

"Like his father?" Faramund asks.

Stella taps her foot again. "Like his father."

Sensing the end of their conversation, Talin slips from the dungeon and tucks himself back behind the door. Stella steps from the shadows of the dungeon, and he watches her disappear down the corridor. He waits for a long while until the palace is still and he's positive his mother isn't nearby. Emerging from his hiding place, he scans the line of windows on the opposite wall, overlooking the courtyard and the darkening horizon. Faint stars are already beginning to speckle the sky. His heart rests at the bottom of his stomach, beating as fast as humanly possible.

"So, she's going to kill me," Talin mutters under his breath. He inhales the scent of the salty river that seeps through the windows. He knows his mother doesn't love him—not like a mother should—but he thought he was at least tolerable. His heart stutters for a moment before slowing down as a thought occurs to him. He smiles slowly, knowing he has the upper hand. He knows their plan—so he can stop it. He's not going to die. Not by the hand of the same man that took his father from him.

He heads back to his room, taking the longest route possible, soaking in the beautiful nature and the tranquility of the coming night. As he breathes in the fresh scent of nature that drifts through the palace on a chilly, end-of-summer breeze, he realizes that he's not afraid. Not anymore. He's content, in a way. After all, this is just another day as the prince of Klymora. He should be used to everything being unexpected.

Talin unlocks the door to his chambers and disappears inside, locking it again. He drags his desk chair over to the door and balances it under the door handle, making it difficult to open.

Talin spins back around and examines his room, taking inventory of his books, his wardrobe, and his practice swords piled in the corner.

He climbs onto his bed, exhausted. Resting his head on his soft pillow, he welcomes sleep. Ignoring every sound and every worry, he drifts away to a land that doesn't want to hurt him.

He knows he's dreaming when he sees Ayne.

"Ayne," Talin whispers, taking her hands in his own. Her eyes are wide with curiosity as she looks at him. "You're beautiful today."

Ayne blushes and glances away. Her hair tumbles from her traditional braid crown and falls across her shoulders. "Thank you, Talin. But why do you say such things?"

Talin shrugs. "I say what I think. Especially around

you. Especially when it's true."

Her cheeks turn rose-red, and her brown eyes flit around the garden before returning to him. She starts to say something, then frowns, creasing her brow. "I—"

"You don't know what to say," Talin interrupts, smirking.

Ayne crosses her arms and huffs. "I'm—"

"Ayne Edelweiss, heiress of Gaia. Yes. I've heard that before."

She practically growls, shoving her nose in the air and speaking to him in a very arrogant tone. "Please, Prince Talin. You can't possibly know what I'm going to say."

Talin touches a slightly wavy strand of her hair and tucks it behind her ear. Her orange day dress brings out the gold in her eyes, as she is aware. The sun is so bright that it turns her black hair a dark brown. "I believe I do. I know you that well."

Ayne lifts a brow. "Surely you aren't serious." A wisp of a smile finds its way to her lips and she attempts to hide it behind her hand—dare Talin see her smile when she's trying so hard to be serious.

Talin brushes her hand aside and tilts her chin up. "I love your smile, Ayne. Please don't hide it."

Ayne holds his eyes for a moment before stepping away, toying with a beautiful white rose on the other side of the path. "What are we going to do, Talin?"

"About what?" he asks, coming up beside her.

She looks over her shoulder at him and frowns. "Your mother is going to have you killed, Talin. You can't exactly ignore that."

He scowls and directs his gaze to his worn shoes. "I was trying not to think about it."

"You have to. We have to come up with a plan. How are you going to outsmart Faramund? He's killed before. He has experience. And with the queen on his side, your chances aren't looking good." She reaches out and rests her hand on his shoulder. "Please, Talin. Be safe. Look out for yourself. I'll help you when I get back."

Talin smiles at the thought of her return. "And when will that be, Ayne?"

She chuckles, bending down to smell a rose. "Sooner than you think."

CHAPTER THREE

The Shadow

T alin wipes the perspiration from his forehead and lunges toward a leg of his poster bed, hacking it with a practice sword. If he's going to defend himself, he has to get better at fighting. A primal sound bellows from his mouth as he spins and lunges again, chipping the wood of his bedpost. He takes a shaky breath and tries again, determined to improve even the slightest bit.

A knock resounds about his chambers. His cotton shirt is stuck to his skin with sweat, and his curly brown hair is flat and grungy. His stomach jumps. "Who is it?" he calls.

"Gladis Dendlewind," she responds. He can already tell she's smiling.

"Wait one second," Talin says, moving his desk chair out of the way and unlocking the door. He throws it open to reveal Miss Dendlewind's twinkling green eyes.

"I brought you breakfast, Your Highness," Miss Dendlewind says, bustling into the room and setting the tray on the end of his bed. She glances around, her eyes lingering on the marked post. She purses her lips, but she chooses to not say anything.

"Oh." Talin rubs his stomach, diving onto his bed and eagerly picking up the silver spoon to dig into his bowl of spiced oats. "Your cooking is unmatched," he swears, taking a bite.

Miss Dendlewind beams. Her puffy cheeks turn rosy. "Why thank you, Prince Talin. Anything for my favorite royal."

He rolls his eyes playfully. "Are you sure it isn't my beloved mother?"

Miss Dendlewind waves his words away. "Tsk. Tsk."

Talin chuckles, finishing his oats. "What are

your plans today, Miss Dendlewind?"

Miss Dendlewind taps her finger on her chin while she ponders his question. "Well, I was thinking about visiting my nephews. Unless you have something you want me to do?" she asks, raising an eyebrow.

Talin shakes his head. "No, no. Have fun with your family. If anyone deserves it, it's you."

Miss Dendlewind smiles at him and turns to leave his chambers, her eyes catching on the chipped bedpost again. She stops and hesitantly asks, "What have you been up to, Your Highness?"

Talin flushes, glancing away. He watches a pair of birds soar through the sky outside his window before answering, "I'm trying to get better at my swordsmanship."

She nibbles on her lip, scanning the rest of the room like she can see all his secrets. "Is there a particular reason, if you don't mind my prying?"

"I arrested Faramund yesterday for the murder of my father."

Miss Dendlewind squeaks in surprise. She takes a step closer. "So, it's true then? It was never an accident?"

"It's true," Talin sighs. "My mother visited his

cell. She gave him another task. But this time, it's my life she wants to end." He barely has enough courage to look at her—at her eyes that are widened in shock and her mouth that's drawn tight in disbelief.

"Your *mother*?" She gulps, wiping her sweaty palms on her dress. "It was Queen Stella all along?"

"Every moment," Talin admits. "I was just too naïve to see it."

"Is there anything I can do? We can't let her kill another great monarch."

Talin stands up from his bed and wraps her in a hug. Her hair smells like blossoms and fresh pastries. "I'm not sure there is anything anyone can do. But if I think of something, I'll tell you right away."

Miss Dendlewind nods. "Thank you. I'll be off now. *Please,* be careful."

Talin watches her as she leaves his chambers. His mask of bravery slips, and he crumbles to the floor. He cries until his throat is dry and his voice is hoarse.

He wipes his face and leaves his chambers, hands balled into white-knuckled fists. His stride is determined and hostile, knowing what he needs to do. He needs to confront the assassin who killed his father and is now coming after him. Talin throws open the door and bounds down the stairs to the dungeon. He stops in front of Faramund's cell and glowers at the assassin.

Faramund's brown eyes pierce him through the shadows. He steps into a sliver of sunlight, illuminating his scowl. "Come to torment me, *Prince* Talin?"

Talin bares his teeth, pulling his dagger from its sheath. Without thinking, he reaches through the cell and grabs a fistful of Faramund's dirty shirt, forcing the prisoner toward the bars. He lifts the blade of his dagger, which glints in the light, to the man's neck.

"Have you come to kill me?" Faramund hisses, reaching through the bars to grab Talin's arms. Instead of trying to force the dagger away from his throat, he digs his nails into the prince's shoulders. "Do you think I deserve to die? I *did* kill your father, after all."

Talin growls, staring into the eyes of his father's murderer, wanting to do nothing else but avenge his father. "Killing you would only be fair—after what you've already done to my family."

"*Fair*," Faramund laughs. Spit flies into Talin's face. "Fair would be to leave me in peace. You've arrested me. You've tormented me. And now you're threatening my life. I just want peace, Your Highness."

Talin barks out a bitter laugh. "*Peace*? A coward like you shall never receive peace!"

"*Go*, Prince Talin. Before something bad happens to you," Faramund insists, his tone implying death.

Talin gulps, flexing his fingers on the handle of his dagger. With one last disdainful glare at Faramund, he releases his shirt and backs away from his cell. Coming down here was foolish. He shouldn't have visited his father's murderer. Talin curses at himself and storms up the steps.

Talin shakes his head as he breaks into the sunlit corridor. He's so lost in his thoughts that he doesn't realize he's gained more company. He glances up right before running into her, and the blood in his veins turns to ice. "Mother?"

Stella glares down at her son, her black nails digging into the fabric on her hips. "What are you doing here, Talin?" Her words are venom.

Talin pales. His palms are clammy, but he

17

refuses to let his mother see how much she frightens him. "Visiting my prisoner. What about you?"

Stella irks an eyebrow. "And what did you two discuss?"

Talin ignores her question. "What are you doing here, Mother?"

She clicks her tongue. "Fine. So be it. I was coming to see Faramund as well. I couldn't believe it when I heard he killed your father." She gasps and glances away. Pinching her eyes closed tightly to drive a tear down her cheek. She doesn't wipe it away. "Faramund. A man who has worked under us for *how* many years? I would never have pegged him for a killer."

Talin stares wide-eyed at her. His mouth falls open, but he quickly snaps it shut. He moves to pass his mother when she stops him with a hand on his shoulder.

"Key?" she asks, looking at him expectantly.

"Lost it," Talin lies, brushing by her. He attempts to keep his pace normal until he's out of her view, and then he runs down the hall, bursting into the garden.

The sun is welcome after the chill of his mother.

CHAPTER FOUR

The Dream

T alin kicks the ground, flinging a chunk of soil and grass into the surrounding brambles. His mother cried! She let that solitary tear slide down her cheek, ensuring he saw it. Her words are meaningless and empty. Surely, Stella's aware that Talin knows she was behind his father's murder. At least that he *suspects* it was her.

Talin collapses to the ground, resting his head on the warm grass and gazing up at the blue sky. He hates that he has to do this alone, wishing, more than anything, that Ayne was here with him. He groans and closes his eyes. He's exhausted. He doesn't want to live every day looking over his shoulder, destroying his bedposts with his sword practice, or lying awake at night, too afraid to sleep —wondering if the shadows in the corners are Faramund, coming to finish him off just like he did his father.

Talin shuts his eyes, finding the vaguest hint of safety in the sunlight. His head is heavy with fatigue, and the grass is perfectly warmed by the sun, so he can't help but fall into a deep slumber and a wonderful dream.

Ayne's warm fingers slip between his. She meets his eyes. Her eyes are full of concern. "So, she lied to you."

"Yes. I'm not surprised," Talin says, raking his fingers through his hair. A stray curl flops across his forehead. "She's been lying to me for years."

"What are you going to do about it? Confront her?" Ayne lifts a dark eyebrow, smirking.

Talin gives her a look. "That'd be crazy. I can't confront her. She wants me killed. I'm not going to make it easier for her." He takes a shallow breath and huffs, "I think it's best if I stay away from her."

"I think that's best too," Ayne replies, twisting her

long black hair into a braid. Her signature gold threads catch in the light. "At least, until you have backup. You definitely can't challenge her on your own. That'd be a death sentence, and I don't want you to get hurt."

Talin nibbles on his bottom lip, trying to not focus on the way the sun plays with her hair or the way it makes the golden flecks in her eyes sparkle. "I miss you, Ayne."

Ayne smiles, tracing slow circles on the back of his hand with her thumb. "I miss you too, Talin. But don't worry. I'm here, and I don't have anywhere else to be."

"What about your family? What about Gaia?" He sighs. "I know you never wanted our marriage. Are you still searching for a way out of it?"

Ayne frowns. "I'm unsure. I suppose, logically thinking, ruling Klymora is a good thing. My sister can rule Gaia. It's just strange. I grew up believing I was going to be the queen of Gaia, only to end up being the queen of Klymora."

Talin tries to squelch the hope flaring inside of him. "Does this mean you're no longer opposed to our marriage?"

Ayne pouts. "I don't want to be married. I knew I would have to, eventually. It just wasn't supposed to be for many years."

"Oh," Talin whispers. "I understand that."

Ayne scoots closer to him. Her long eyelashes cast shadows on her cheeks. "I don't want you to feel disappointed."

Talin shakes his head. "You could never disappoint me, Ayne."

A melodic laugh slips from between her lips as she lays back in the grass. "If that were truly the case, you wouldn't be frowning."

Talin sighs, forcing himself to smile. "You could never disappoint me, Ayne. Is that better?"

Ayne bats at him playfully. "Much better."

"Are you going to help me?" Talin can't help but ask. His curiosity courses through every syllable.

Ayne extends her pinky finger. "I promise."

Talin wakes up and blinks at the silver clouds above him and the hazy moon in his peripheral. He yawns, stretches, and glances around. His back is sore from sleeping on the ground. He half expects someone to be waiting for him, hunting him down, glaring at him from the shadows—but he can sense without further inspection that he's alone.

He stands up and dusts off his pants. His arms are sore, and his movements are strained. When he heads back into the palace, his only companion is the lone owl hooting in a nearby tree. Talin pauses to listen to the sound. The owl pauses then too, as if it knows it has an audience. Talin glances around. A thick, lone tree branch sways in the night, and a pair of large yellow eyes stare back at him.

Talin lifts his hand in a small wave, and the snow-white owl glances away.

"I'd be scared too," Talin whispers, stirring the silence. "I bet I look awful. You, however, are quite a beautiful creature—for sleeping outside, I mean." He chuckles, realizing he's talking to a creature that can't even reply.

The owl peers at him wearily before leaving its post on the branch for the chill of the ledge. This corridor has half-walls on either side. It's open to nature, except for an occasional stone pillar. Talin steps back in surprise, before extending a hand to brush the creature's feathers. The owl doesn't seem to mind.

"Very beautiful indeed," Talin purrs.

CHAPTER FIVE

The Meeting

T alin lowers to his chest, squinting through the weathered floorboards. He grins mischievously—so Miss Dendlewind is right. He *can* see straight into the dungeon from here.

The abandoned guest chamber he's in smells musty and stale since it's directly above the dungeon. He imagines the screams of the prisoners would be rather loud up here, which is why his mother only gives the unwelcome guests this room. His eyes fall to the dust motes highlighted by the sunlight coming through the tall window, before returning his gaze to the assassin below. He blinks, pressing closer as the door beneath opens and slams closed. He can see his mother as she saunters toward the prisoner. Her sleek brown hair swishes with her movement. Talin scowls. *What does she want now?*

"Faramund," Stella drawls, wrapping her hands around the bars. Faramund stands up, leveling his eyes at the queen. "How is life in the shadows?"

Faramund scoffs, running a hand down his face. "I've always lived in the shadows, my queen. This is no different."

Stella sighs and pulls back, fumbling with something in the pouch at her side. She reveals a key, glinting in the thin light stretching from the broken floorboards of the guest chamber. She twists it in the lock and the cell opens.

Talin gasps and presses the pocket of his long navy coat. He can still feel Faramund's key in his pocket. So, how does *she* have it?

"I thought Talin had the key?" Faramund says, refusing to move from the middle of his cell.

"Not the *only* key." She takes a step closer to him, her hand perched on her hip. "Why are you still standing there?"

Faramund shakes his head. "I thought this was over."

"It's not. Talin is just a hiccup," Stella insists, embracing the grungy assassin. "You know how I feel about you. Do you not feel the same?"

Faramund hesitates a second longer before melting into her embrace. "I've always felt the same, my queen."

"Love," Stella purrs, bringing his hand to her cheek. "You used to address me as your love. I like that one more."

Talin can barely see the two in the shadows as they inch farther and farther into the cell—the sounds of passionate kissing and empty promises churn his stomach.

He can barely believe what he's seeing. His mother is locked in a lover's embrace with his father's murderer. He can't stand it anymore. He pushes off the floor and practically runs from the guest chamber. His footsteps echo through the hallway, bouncing off the rough stone walls and startling a maid who's sweeping the entrance to the dining hall. She watches Talin as he storms by, tossing open the doors to the back garden. He lets them slam behind him, not caring who hears.

Talin rakes his hands through his hair, leaving disheveled curls bouncing against his forehead. The sun is high in the sky, painting the lush grass golden. The golden color is yet another reminder of his short-term guest and fiancée: *Ayne.* He frowns down at his feet. The leather fronts of his shoes are worn; there's a hole in the making. He probably should buy a new pair—but shoes, of all things, aren't on the forefront of his mind.

"Please come back," he whispers, staring across the garden and toward the location of the elm tree. A murder of crows caw in a nearby tree, and his frown deepens. "I *need* you, Ayne."

CHAPTER SIX

The Discussion

W e aren't going to war with Zhongguo," Stella declares, staring daggers at the nobles across the dining table from her. "I want you all to stop spreading that rumor."

Talin peeks up from his docile façade, wanting to see how many disagree with what she's saying— or how many want to say something in response but are too afraid. He doesn't want to poke the bear, per se, so he thought it might be best to remain quiet. But now...he can't let his mother bully all these people into thinking the same things as her, no matter if they're factual or not. "They can't just be rumors, Mother."

Stella turns her laser-sharp attention to her son, tapping a claw on the table. A smirk pulls at her lips. "Emperor Neo and I have sent several letters regarding the notion. He was going to wage war against us just because he wanted more land." She huffs and tucks a loose strand of brown hair behind her ear. "But ever since the inclusion of Rutheria, he's changed his mind. Rutheria is searching for a special flower that can heal any disease, and that flower is somewhere in Zhongguo. Emperor Neo doesn't want those fools tearing apart his land, so he's asked us..." she rolls her eyes, "and Gaia, to form a sort of alliance."

"Are we sending our militia to Zhongguo then?" Cedric Hemmingway asks, tilting his head. His suit is crisp and ironed, not a stitch out of place.

Stella inclines her head toward him. "No, we're not. Not yet, anyway. He's going to try to handle things on his side, but if Rutheria gets violent—we'll send a small militia to Zhongguo to help."

"Why are we doing this for someone who was going to try to steal our land?" another noble asks.

His tone implies that Stella hasn't a clue what she's doing.

She stands up, slapping a hand on the table as her chair squeaks against the floor. "So he *doesn't* steal our land. These are the kind of things you need to do to rule a kingdom," she hisses. "None of you will *ever* understand that."

A few eyes flicker in Talin's direction, and he doesn't miss the underlying meaning of what his mother said: *he'll never make it to the throne.* For an odd reason, though, it doesn't send a shiver down his spine. It doesn't scare him at all. He knows his mother is evil and that she'd go to desperate measures to ensure she's in charge... Ayne even warned him.

He peers down at the table, wondering if Ayne received his letters... What did she think? What is she doing right now? He sighs, resting his elbow on the table and his chin in his hand. *I wish, more than anything, that you were here.*

A knock sounds about the dining hall, and a guard positioned on one side of the door turns to open it. He disappears outside to deal with the person; interrupting a royal meeting is incredibly frowned upon and is punishable by any means the queen deems fit. The only exception, however, is if the kingdom is at stake.

Murmurs rise among the nobles, but Talin ignores them. It's probably no one. A maid, perhaps.

"Your Majesty," the guard calls, peeking back in from the corridor. Stella's head darts up, catching his urgent tone.

"What is it?" she demands, narrowing her eyes at him.

He gestures to the corridor. "You have a guest."

She bristles and sweeps her hand toward the table, a menacing smile tight on her lips, prepared to make a fool of whoever interrupted them. "Send them in."

The guard goes moon-white. "As you say, Your Majesty."

The door swings open, and Stella's pallor matches the guard's. Several nobles' heads swivel toward the guest, mouths wide open, eyes as big as dinner plates. Curiosity pulls Talin's attention toward the person, wondering why his mother isn't bellowing for the gallows already.

Then…when he sees her…his heart nearly stops.

She smiles over at him, her head held high.

She's wearing a sunshine yellow dress with a high collar and white stitching down her bodice. Her sleeves are long and translucent, showing her tanned skin underneath.

Her eyes sparkle. "Hello, Talin."

Talin gulps then runs his suddenly sweaty hands down his pant legs. "Ayne?"

CHAPTER SEVEN

Her Return

"A yne," Talin says for what feels like the millionth time, still in disbelief. He glances over at her just to make sure she's *really* here. Her breath-taking smile stuns him, and he stops walking, right in the middle of the path. The once-blooming flowers around him are now shriveled; autumn has come.

"Talin," Ayne responds, chuckling. Her hair is swept up into a braid crown with a few strands of gold laced in. "Why are you staring at me?"

His mouth is suddenly dry. He breaks into an awkward grin and runs a hand through his hair, staring at anything besides her. "Did you, by chance, receive my letters?"

Ayne doesn't answer. She's scowling when he finally gains enough courage to look her way again. "Ayne?"

"I never got a chance to read them all, unfortunately," she says, shaking her head. "A lot was going on over there."

"Oh... That's fine. There wasn't anything important in them," he insists. Though, inside, he's very disappointed. He poured his feelings onto those pages and she never finished reading them? "What happened over there? I only know bits and pieces."

Her eyes dull. "Many things."

"You don't have to explain. I heard about the rebels, the fire, and the so-called witch betraying her country." Talin starts walking again, gesturing for her to follow. "That was quite an appearance you made back there."

Ayne, after a momentary pause, breaks into a smile. "I thought I would try to save you from the meeting."

"I'm glad you did," Talin admits, smirking at

her. Her face turns pink. He takes that as a success. "So where's your little mouse?"

Ayne bumps into his shoulder, sending him into a fit of laughter. "He's *not* a mouse. He's a gerbil! And right now, he's with my sister in Gaia."

"If you say so," Talin retorts, earning himself another bump to the shoulder. When they finally reach the end of the path, he pushes the stringy dead bushes out of the way to reveal the elm tree, wilting from autumn.

Ayne claps a hand on his shoulder, awestruck. "You brought me back here."

"It is our place, after all," Talin says.

She smiles so big it reaches her eyes, making them glitter tenfold. "It is. Thank you, Talin."

Talin grabs hold of his courage and takes her hand, intertwining his fingers with hers. He pulls her toward the tree. Astoundingly, she doesn't let go.

When they're underneath the elm tree, Talin leans back and stares straight up into the thinning branches, bright sunshine cuts through the exposed spaces.

"It's beautiful, even when it's losing its leaves," Ayne says in wonder.

Talin starts, "So are you..." He realizes too late

what he implied.

"Talin?" Ayne says, drawing his attention and preventing him from stammering even more. "I think I know what you meant."

He meets her eyes, smiling fondly, thankful that she understands him. "It's true."

She rubs the pad of her thumb across the back of his hand. "Thank you." She pulls him down to take a seat at the tree's roots. "Now tell me about your life. What happened while I was away?" She crosses her legs politely under her dress, lifting an eyebrow in question.

Talin takes a steadying breath. How much should he tell her? He decides that the only true option is...telling her everything. So, he does.

CHAPTER EIGHT

The Maid

Ayne's standing at the cliffside, glaring down at the port. She crosses her arms and growls, "She cannot do this."

Talin steps up behind her, tentatively taking her by the elbow and spinning her toward him. Ayne's expression softens when her eyes land on him. "I'm afraid she can. Though, the execution of a prince would be a pretty big scandal if word got around."

"So, let's spread the word. She'd never go through with it if everyone was keeping a close eye on her," Ayne says, tapping her foot in the grass as her mind races.

Talin shrugs. "You may be right. Then it *would* be suspicious if I did die—and she'd get the blame."

"Don't say that," Ayne insists, furrowing her brow.

"Say what?" Talin asks.

"You're not going anywhere. Don't even consider that as a possibility." She shakes her head sternly as if that's the end of *this* conversation.

"I'll have Miss Dendlewind spread the word. It'll be more believable coming from a maid. They *do* hear everything," Talin suggests.

"Good idea," Ayne adds, nodding. She turns back to face the palace. "It seems a lifetime ago that I was here. Is it odd that I'm relieved to be back?"

"Not at all," Talin says. "I'm happy you're back."

Ayne toys with a loose strand of hair, a wisp of a smile forming on her face. "I'm glad. So, shall we go tell Miss Dendlewind?"

Talin beams. "I think we shall."

Ayne pushes open the door to her old guest chambers—the same one she's supposed to keep when she moves into the palace, a change that's destined to happen in the coming weeks. What would other countries think if the fiancée of a prince lived in a different country and slept in a different palace? Normally, she'd protest. But she has to keep up appearances, for her own sake and her family's. And this way, she can watch Talin's back.

Miss Dendlewind is dusting the bookshelf, humming a sweet tune. She glances over her shoulder when the door creaks open, then does a double-take when she realizes who it is. She tosses the feather duster over her shoulder and onto the floor, pulling Ayne into her arms. "Princess! Where have you been?"

Ayne squeaks from inside a Miss Dendlewind cocoon, "I was in Zhongguo on business."

Miss Dendlewind releases Ayne from her hug, pinning her at arm's length. "Well, I'm glad you're back." She sweeps up a loose strand of hair and tucks it into Ayne's braid. "And I like your hair. It's very befitting of you."

Ayne peeks over at Talin, then bites her lip as she says, "Miss Dendlewind. Talin and I have a favor to ask."

Miss Dendlewind cocks her head. "Anything for you two."

"Would you spread something throughout the palace? Tell anyone—*everyone*."

"I'm not keen on starting rumors, Princess Ayne," Miss Dendlewind says, already shaking her head.

"It's not exactly a rumor. It's a precaution for my safety," Talin jumps in, speaking with his hands. "If you do this for me, I'll be forever in your debt."

Miss Dendlewind meets his eyes for a brief moment, debating whether or not to accept his offer. She folds. "As I said, anything for you two. Now, what is it that you want me to say?"

Ayne gestures to the end of the bed, taking a seat. She crosses her legs and rests her hands on her knees. "Queen Stella and Faramund are responsible for the death of King Archibald, as Talin already told you. But Queen Stella isn't going to stop at just King Archibald. She's coming after Talin, and we think we know a way to stop her," she explains.

Miss Dendlewind's green eyes widen, and her round face scrunches with concern. "What have you come up with? I'll say anything to help Prince

Talin."

"I'm glad we can count on you," Ayne says, beaming at the maid. "Tell everyone who'll listen that Queen Stella and Faramund the Assassin are plotting to kill Prince Talin. Do this for us, please."

Miss Dendlewind knits her brows and sets her lips. She nods. "Alright, Princess Ayne. I'll do it. Word will erupt like wildfire—there won't be a soul in Caledonia who doesn't know by morning."

Ayne nods, and Miss Dendlewind gets up, snatches the feather duster, and heads toward the door with a fierce look of determination. She stops with her hand around the knob, then smiles over her shoulder at the princess. "Welcome back, Princess Ayne. This kingdom is lucky to have you." She twists open the door and disappears down the hallway, her long pale blue dress swishing against the floor.

"She's right," Talin whispers, watching the open doorway. "We are very lucky to have you." He rests his hand over Ayne's, relishing the warmth of her touch. "Thank you for coming back."

Her golden-specked eyes widen, falling from his face down to their hands. "Of course I'm back. I have obligations, Talin. A princess doesn't just run away from…everything."

Talin removes his hand from hers, standing briskly from the end of the bed. Obligations… Is that all he is to her? An obligation? He frowns, sweeping his left arm toward the chambers. "These are yours still, Ayne. I'll be in my chambers if you need me—ask one of the maids for directions." He crosses his hands behind his back and leaves her chambers, letting his head hang as soon as he's out of sight.

Obligations…

CHAPTER NINE

The Planner

I s it true?" a maid whispers, glancing up from her task of sweeping the hallway. The maid beside her polishing the stonework chances a look at the prince as he walks by.

"You know the queen *would* do something like that..." she mutters, darting her eyes back to the rag in her hand when Talin shifts, peeking at the two over his shoulder.

"Yes, she very much would," the first maid says, clicking her tongue as she drags the broom across the floor. "Poor prince. He was turning out to be just like his father."

"A good man," the second maid adds, shaking her head solemnly. "I hope Queen Stella doesn't go through with it. How evil can a mother be to want her son dead?"

Talin, far enough away now that their conversation fades to comfortable background noise, sighs. Ayne's plan has worked so far. And Miss Dendlewind, the ever-impressive woman, has spread the word of the threat quicker than either of them could've anticipated. However, what will his mother do once she hears the servants' mumblings? He hopes she doesn't hurt them... The servants don't deserve to be punished.

Talin frowns, turning the corner toward his chambers. He stops ten paces away, eyes as wide as dinner plates and heart stampeding as fast as a horse.

"What do you want?" he practically growls, glaring at the figure standing in front of his door.

His mother frowns, tears beading on her waterlines. She shakes her head at her son. "I'm so sorry, Talin. I just heard."

Talin steals another step toward his mother.

"Heard what?" he asks, furrowing his brow. *Did she hear the servants chattering already?*

Stella waves him forward. He reluctantly does as she requests, standing a mere arm's length away. "Your father's killer, Talin, he escaped."

Talin forgets to act shocked. "Faramund is gone?" His voice is deadpan like he expected just this. Which, of course, he did—how can Talin be assassinated, if the assassin is behind bars?

Stella nods, blinking a tear from her eye. "Yes. I went down there just a little bit ago, and the guards said he fought past them. That he's no longer in the dungeon." She lets a tiny whimper escape—how very un-Stella-like. "He has to be hiding somewhere in the palace."

"Are you going to go after him, Mother?" Talin asks, not believing for a second that she didn't have something to do with Faramund's escape.

Stella pulls her son into a hug. Talin's so startled that he doesn't pull away. "We'll figure something out, darling." The warmth of her embrace is cruel... How dare she pretend to care when he knows that Queen Stella is incapable of caring. Her heart is made of ice and only a chisel made of violence can break through it.

His eyes start to sting. He's longed for his mother's affection. How devastating is it that she finally embraces him after coordinating his assassination?

Talin lets his hands fall to his sides. Maybe they were too late. Maybe the rumors won't save him now.

"Meanwhile," Stella continues, ignorant to his inner turmoil, "since Princess Ayne has returned from whatever task her parents sent her on, it's about time we've finalized the marriage between you both."

Talin bites his cheek. "That's still happening? But what about the alliance between Klymora, Gaia, and Zhongguo? Wouldn't our marriage be pointless now?"

Stella clicks her tongue. "Think like a *king*, Talin. The marriage between you and Ayne can only do good. We'll inherit everything she does. It'll strengthen the alliance with Gaia—at least, it'll appear so for onlookers—and it'll quell our subjects' worries. A wedding right now would be perfect. It'll give everyone something else to focus on instead of the turmoil across the Cari." She rests her hand on her son's shoulder, grinning from ear to ear. "I want you to meet with Miss Luvenia, the royal wedding planner I've commissioned to organize the ceremony."

With nothing else to say, Talin asks, "When do you want us to meet with her?"

Stella's smile grows. "In an hour. She'll be waiting in the empty guest chambers on the first floor. You know which one I'm talking about." Something flickers in her gaze, but as soon as it appears, it's gone.

Talin goes statute-still as his mother passes him, humming a terrible lullaby under her breath. He remembers the song from when he was a child, and the lyrics that accompanied it always sent chills down his spine and nightmares into his sleep.

How did Stella find out about him spying? What is she going to do, now that her and Faramund's affair is no longer a secret? A thin sheen of cold sweat coats his skin as, finally, the full scope of his mother's deception hits him. Instead of entering his room, he turns back around and heads down the hallway, staring at the floor, wondering which method Faramund will use to end him. Halfway toward the open section of the palace, where the beautiful owl had perched the other night, he runs straight into Ayne.

She squeaks, backs up, and rubs the sore spot on her forehead from their collision. She attempts to smile, unsure of what foot she and Talin stand on. "Talin, I didn't mean to hurt your feelings. We have a lot to talk about, don't we?" She smiles bashfully. The sunlight cloaks her right side.

Talin can't help but brighten by her presence alone. "We do. I'm glad I ran into you." He chuckles at his use of words. "My mother is demanding we meet with Miss Luvenia to organize our wedding. She says now is the best time to go through with it." He wants to reach out and pull Ayne into a hug when her face creases with worry. He hates that all this is his fault. His mother wouldn't have latched onto the idea of their marriage if he hadn't insisted upon it. He thought, at the time, that he was doing what was best for Ayne. Cedric Hemmingway is too conceited to become her husband, let alone a *prince*. And who knows how Ayne would've been treated by him... He thought he was saving her from a lifetime of cruelty, when really, he was just trapping her.

"When does she want us to meet with Miss Luvenia?" Ayne asks, plastering a stoic expression on her face. He wants to tell her not to do that, not to hide behind a mask when she's with him.

"In an hour." He can't help himself, reaching out and tucking a strand of her hair behind her ear. His hand lingers above her cheek for far too long, wanting to touch her. "You don't want to marry me, do you?" He cringes as his voice cracks.

Ayne glances away. "I don't know," she finally says. "You would make a good husband. And you'd make a wonderful king. But I never imagined myself getting married at *thirteen*. I know royalty gets married at all sorts of ages, especially when the alliance benefits their kingdoms, but I never saw this as *my* path."

He gives in, cupping her face and bringing her eyes up to meet his. Her cheeks swathe pink, and his heart thumps quickly. "Our marriage doesn't have to be traditional. We don't have to do anything married people do. It'll just be a communion between our kingdoms, a solidification of our friendship."

She gives him a look. "I think a *marriage* is very different from a friendship, Talin."

"Ours doesn't have to be," he promises. "I mean it, Ayne."

She steps away from his touch, running a hand

down the stitching of her dress. "I'll think about it, Talin. I have *a lot* of things to think about." Her expression is haunted.

"Are you okay?" he asks as they start their walk toward the empty guest chambers where Miss Luvenia will be. The same room he was spying through the floorboards in yesterday. Many things can be a coincidence, but *that*, however, cannot. He decides to dwell on that later. Right now, he needs to focus on Ayne.

Ayne walks with her head down, strands of her hair hiding her face from view. He wants nothing more than to quell her worries, to carry the weight of whatever burdens her. "I think I should show you something, Talin. It may be best to just…have it out in the open." She glances at him sheepishly, biting her bottom lip.

He slows his pace, curiosity stealing his attention. "What is it, Ayne?"

She stops a few feet in front of him, her skirt still swishing on the floor. She wrings her hands, glances around, and freezes when a maid comes wandering down the hall, fresh towels draped across her arms and a rather bored expression donning her features. "On second thought, it'd be best to show you some other time. Where no one can observe," Ayne admits as soon as the maid is out of earshot.

Talin chides himself for the rush of disappointment he feels. But he can't help it. Ayne is such a mystery to him; it'd be refreshing to finally unveil at least *one* secret.

They continue walking in silence until they arrive at the door to the guest chambers, where Miss Luvenia is expected to be.

They exchange an unsure look before Talin pushes open the door. They step into the darkness. At first, his heart jumps into his throat. The shadows surrounding him turn alive, creeping toward him with promises of death—each resembling either Faramund or his mother. Skeletal fingers reach toward him, and whispered promises of demise slither across his skin, raising the hair along his arms. He gasps and stumbles back into Ayne, who grunts as she pushes him away. Then the torches in sconces along the wall begin to light, one-by-one. Achingly slow. *Dispel the monsters*, Talin mentally cries, gritting his teeth until he can finally see the woman in the room, holding a lit candle. He releases a breath. *It's not his mother*. The woman eyes him quizzically, placing the candle on the table once all the torches are lit. She tosses open the dusty blue curtains that cover the solitary window, allowing sunlight to fall across the floorboards and onto a tiny table that's covered with a notebook and sticks of charcoal.

"You must be Miss Luvenia?" Talin asks, stepping toward the woman. She's thin with waist-length blonde hair and a peculiarly green pair of eyes. A few fine wrinkles crease her face, but there's a certain ageless beauty that encompasses her. She has a long, regale nose that's straight and perfectly divides her face. And her lips are blush pink and thin.

She smiles, displaying a narrow gap between her front teeth. "Yes, and you're Prince Talin and Princess Ayne? It's a pleasure to plan your wedding. I'm sure Queen Stella would want us to start right away, skip the pleasantries and all that." She speaks quickly like she's trying to push out every word in a single breath. "Come over here, Your Highnesses." She waves them over to a sitting area—three chairs surrounding a small table—and takes a seat. She picks up the notebook and claims a piece of charcoal. She looks at them from under her pale eyelashes expectantly, as if they should know every detail of their ceremony already.

"Well, where to begin..." Ayne starts in a strained voice, tentatively settling down into one of the chairs around the table.

"With the bride, perhaps," Miss Luvenia declares. "What dress are you going to wear? We can design something custom if you want."

"I've always planned on wearing my mother's wedding dress, though I doubt it'll fit me." Ayne looks down at herself with a frown, and Talin can tell what she's thinking. How she should be eighteen, not *thirteen*.

"Alterations can be made so it'll fit you," Miss Luvenia suggests, scribbling something hastily down in her notebook. She glances back up at Ayne eagerly.

Ayne grimaces but nods—an answer which, surprisingly, Miss Luvenia accepts. Miss Luvenia continues to scribble in her notebook. Then she turns to Talin, eyebrows retreating into her hairline when he doesn't speak right away. "And you? What suit will you be wearing?"

"Um." Talin scrunches his nose, deciding that he should be mature about this because if he wasn't, word would get back to his mother. But why does he care? His mother is trying to have him killed. Let her choke on stories of her immature son. "I was considering something a little more...*newsworthy*."

Miss Luvenia waves her hand for him to continue, but by the crease between her brows, he knows she's one to stand on the more traditional side.

"So," Talin rests his forearms on the table and leans toward Miss Luvenia, "if I was buck naked, do you think that would be a wedding to remember?"

Miss Luvenia gapes at him with horror, but Ayne's bell-like laughter tells him he took the right approach.

"Be civil, Prince Talin. What you say will make its way back to your mother. She *does* have to approve everything before I can begin," Miss Luvenia warns, looking aghast.

Talin smirks, tilting his head to the side, a lone curl flopping against his temple. "Then take note that the meal should be pheasant—raw and flapping. The flower arrangements should only be daffodils, and as for the guests, write down that no one is coming; a small, unpublicized affair between families." He stands up, pride swelling in his chest when he takes in her shell-shocked expression. "As for you, Miss Luvenia, I'm sorry if you were relying on the monetary income from planning this event, but you will no longer be needed."

He exits the room with his hands in his pockets and a grin on his face. For once, he feels in control of his life.

CHAPTER TEN

The Idea

Ayne's footsteps quicken as she tries to catch up to Talin. She huffs, padding next to him. Talin doesn't even react, a glowing grin is cemented on his face. He stops in the center of the open corridor, the tree branch swaying at eye level is now void of the beautiful owl. He spins toward her with his hands on his hips.

"What happened in there?" Ayne asks, watching him with perplexed, sparkling eyes.

Talin runs a hand through his hair, fixing his

stray curls. "I realized something."

"What did you realize?" Ayne presses, tilting her head. Her black hair tumbles over her shoulder, strands of gold glinting in the sunlight. "I certainly hope it has nothing to do with a newfound fascination with nudity."

Talin chuckles, shaking his head. "Not my thing. But I realized that I'm not going to live under the thumb of my mother anymore. She's trying to have me killed—she already freed Faramund—so I'm done playing the part of a perfect prince."

Ayne's expression slackens at the mention of Faramund's freedom. "What are you going to do?"

"I'm going to live. I'm going to get rid of Faramund and my mother. I'm going to take over this kingdom and become king." Talin pounds his fist against his flat palm, determination sparked with each word. He deflates a bit. "But I still have to figure out all the nitty-gritty details."

"I'll help you figure them out," Ayne offers, continuing down the hallway with her hands behind her back.

Talin trails after her, his mind a mess of questions and ideas; a puzzle missing a piece.

Ayne leads them to the kitchen; the same one

57

they ate in all those nights ago. The sunlight now paints the floor and counters golden. The scent of rosemary and melted cheese rides on the gentle breeze, and the busy chatter of cooks welcomes them. Ayne pushes open the door, takes a deep breath, and grins at the head cook when he comes over to introduce himself.

"I'm Jacque. And you must be Princess Ayne Edelweiss?" Jacque juts his hand toward her. His rutty face has fading scars from the war between Klymora and Gaia; he only returned from the field after Ayne and Talin's engagement was announced, bringing a stop to the war. "And our dear Prince Talin, how are you?" He bites his cheek and leans down. "I heard the rumors. Are they true?"

Talin touches the cook's arm casually, stepping around him and deeper into the kitchen. "Yes, they're true—"

"Which is why we came here," Ayne interrupts, releasing Jacque's scarred hand. "We were hoping to find some privacy so we could talk. Plans and counterplans, you see."

Jacque turns and gestures to the two other cooks in the kitchen. They're both rather plump ladies with flour dashed aprons and neat brown buns tight on their heads. They drop their knives onto their cutting blocks and leave the room.

Jacque smiles down at Ayne, gesturing to a small round table in the corner of the room. "Please, do make yourselves comfortable. Luckily for you, dinner doesn't need to be made for a couple more hours. I'll whip something up for you both while you scheme."

Ayne and Talin settle into the two chairs beside the table. Ayne tents her fingers and smiles slyly. "I thought we could use a place without your mother's hired ears around." She clears her throat and sighs. "*What* are we going to do?"

Talin bites his lower lip, thoughts already churning in his head, bandaging over the impossibilities and impracticalities and presenting him with clear, polished ideas. "We exile them both."

Ayne gasps, sitting up straight. "*Exile*?"

"That's the only way we can get rid of them both. We can't hurt them, and we can't imprison them, but with all the suspicion surrounding my mother right now, we might have a shot. at convincing the court to exile them."

Ayne takes his hand, which he didn't know was shaking. "But that means you'll have to take the throne…"

Talin levels his gaze with her, his mouth pressed into a stern line. "I know. I don't see another way."

Ayne chews on his words carefully. "Are you ready for that kind of responsibility? You're going to be turning *fifteen* in five months."

"I'm going to have to be." Talin tries for a convincing smile, but falls short. "I'll have help from the court, the servants, and my people. I can free the servants, completely end the war between our kingdoms, and we won't have to go through with our marriage." Even though his heart beats quicker at the sound of Ayne's voice, and the thought of marrying her is a pleasant one, he knows this is what's right for both of them. They're too young to wed, to make such a commitment. He needs to focus on his people and his kingdom.

Ayne gapes at him. "Everything will be solved…" She takes her hand back when Jacque brings over a plate of steaming bread halves dribbled with olive oil and sprinkled with parsley. The smell alone makes Talin's mouth water. "When should we present the idea to the court?"

Talin selects a piece of bread and tears a chunk off with his fingers. The oil from the bread drips onto the tabletop. Once he swallows, he says, "I have two things I need to do first." He stands up, his chair legs squeaking on the floor. "I'll see you tomorrow evening. Underneath the elm at sunset?"

Ayne's eyes widen with curiosity. She nods. "I'll see you there. I have to go back to my kingdom for the night. I'll have my things brought over tomorrow. But I'd hate to leave you alone with everything that is going on." She stands up too. "Are you sure you'll be fine tonight? Lock your door and keep the torches lit."

Talin smiles at her concern, a blush creeping up his neck and painting the tips of his ears. He knows it's nothing like *that*, it's just *Ayne*; the protector. "I'll be safe. Okay?"

She reluctantly nods, doubt still apparent in her expression.

CHAPTER ELEVEN

The Training

Ayne circles Talin, raising a wooden staff in the air. The breeze drifting over the cliffside and across the salty Abhainn River tugs her hair loose from her braid. Stray strands flutter over her shoulders. Caz squeaks from his perch on a tree root, protesting against the cold.

Ayne swings the staff, sliding her foot forward while bending her other knee. Her staff hits Talin in the calf, and he winces, frowning at her.

"Why did you want to beat me up again?" he

asks, rubbing a sore spot on his chest from the last time her staff found its mark.

"I'm not *just* beating you up," Ayne exclaims. Her cheeks are rosy from the exertion. She's always appreciated the training her father put her through—though it's minimal at best. "I'm teaching you how to defend yourself—if only you actually *raised* your staff."

Talin glares at her. "I don't want to hurt you, though—"

"Pretend I'm an enemy then," Ayne insists, refusing to acknowledge the blush creeping up her neck. She forces herself to meet his soft blue eyes. "Pretend I'm Faramund. Or your mother." She raises a thin, black eyebrow. "Or even Cedric Hemmingway."

Talin gives her a begrudging look, but finally lifts his staff, taking a step toward her. He matches her movement, and their staffs clink. He hops back as Ayne quickly swings her staff toward his ankles, hoping to knock him off balance again. His butt still hurts from the last time she made him fall to the ground. "I'd rather just picture you as Ayne—" he says, his breath slightly labored. If he's being honest, he's never exerted himself so much at once.

Traveling in a cushioned carriage or standing at a podium in front of people doesn't require that much energy. Defending himself—that's a different story.

Talin huffs, jumping to the side when Ayne passes her staff between her hands and tries to hit him in the side. He doesn't even think she's trying to be gentle.

"Are you *trying* to kill me?" he asks, though he knows she's not. She's trying to train him to defend himself so that Faramund *doesn't* kill him. But jeez... He gently rubs the spot on his arm where her staff collided with his skin. That's definitely going to bruise. "I'm going to be purple and blue tomorrow."

Ayne grins, finally letting up. She rests her staff on the ground and leans her cheek against the worn wood. Her eyes sparkle. "I think a few bruises are the least you have to worry about."

Talin drops his staff to the ground and plops down, staring across the river toward the sandy dunes of Gaia. He wipes sweat from his forehead with the dirty hem of his sleeve and sighs. "Yeah. You're right."

She sits down next to him, fanning out the light blue skirt of her day dress. "I usually am."

He gives her a sidelong look at that remark, and

they both burst into a chorus of laughter, watching the sun turn the Abhainn River a golden orange.

"Tonight, at dinner, I'm going to set our plan into motion," Talin says softly, hating to disrupt the tranquil moment with mentions of his mother and their plan. "Though it's going to require us to return to Miss Luvenia." He frowns. "After my outburst last time, I don't know how my mother is going to take it when I request that she returns."

Ayne nods in agreement. "It'll be challenging, but we need to do this. If we're going to exile your mother and Faramund, we need to catch them by surprise. Which means you need to act like you usually do—and I need to be less defiant, I suppose."

Talin's head hurts just thinking about the amount of deception ahead of them. Is it even possible to exile the queen? He will have to read over Klymora's laws again, just to make sure their plan stands a chance. But if it does...then they'll finally be free from Stella's cruelty.

"See you later then?" Ayne asks, smiling at him, though her brow is creased with worry.

Talin nods. "See you later, Ayne."

CHAPTER TWELVE

The Friend

M iss Dendlewind glances around the corridor skeptically. Her slightly wavy hair hangs loose around her shoulders, and she's wearing a light gray dress with a lacy white accent stitched around the collar and sleeve cuffs. She finally spots Talin, lurking by the doors of the dining hall, where Queen Stella—along with the rest of the present nobles—are gathered half an hour early for dinner. Mindless chatter drifts through the wide-open doors.

Talin ducks into the shadows when a maid walks by.

He finally looks up and notices Miss Dendlewind. He smiles rather hesitantly. "I'm glad you received my message."

Miss Dendlewind sidles up next to him, half concealed in the darkness, half caught in the sunlight slanting down from a window opposite her. "What can I help you with, Prince Talin? And why are we meeting..." she glances around and shrugs, "here?" Her calm green eyes flick from the dining hall to the prince.

"The second part of my plan is waiting in there," he nods toward the doorway. "I need to request something of you again."

Miss Dendlewind purses her lips, listening furtively. "Do continue."

"The rumors about my mother spread wonderfully—nearly everyone has heard. But it's not enough. Can I ask you to do it again?" He doesn't like asking Miss Dendlewind to do something she's uncomfortable with—such as spreading rumors and tales around the palace—but he needs her to for his plan to work. His heart pounds in his chest as he waits for her response, anxious that someone will step out of the dining hall and overhear their conversation. Miss Dendlewind dips her head in a resolute nod.

"I'm going to need a new story, Prince Talin, if my connections are going to stop their busy work and listen," she explains, offering him a small smile.

"Tell them about my mother and Faramund's affair, and how they were spotted *rendezvousing* in the shadows of the dungeon." Miss Dendlewind gasps as her eyes widen. Talin continues, "Don't forget to mention that he escaped—suggest that she may have had something to do with it." Talin takes a slow breath and nibbles keenly on his bottom lip, eyes flicking between a server supporting a tray of drinks and Miss Dendlewind's thoughtful gaze. "Will you do it?"

Miss Dendlewind sighs, dropping her eyes to the floor. "Of course, I will, Prince Talin. But I'd hate to be known as a gossip—as that person everyone turns to for a drop of drama and scandal. I'm not that kind of lady."

"And I'd never want you to be mistaken as that. When everything is finished, I'll make sure you don't have to do anything like this again," Talin assures her, taking his friend's hand in his own.

Miss Dendlewind smiles warmly. He hates doing this to her, but he *needs* her right now. He *needs* her so he and Ayne can be free and the whole kingdom can thrive.

"Shall I start immediately?" she asks.

Talin glances back at the dining hall, his heart thundering in his chest. If his plan works—if his mother doesn't suspect a thing—then he and Ayne will have their entire futures ahead of them. For once, he won't be under the thumb of his mother. "That would be best."

Miss Dendlewind drops into a curtsey, against the protest of Prince Talin, and scurries back down the hallway in search of willing ears and big mouths.

Talin smooths his sweaty palms down his pants, runs his fingers through his hair, and plasters an approachable smile on his face. A few more nobles wander past him, heading for their seats; their coattails flap behind them as they walk.

Talin slips into the seat to the left of his mother. At first, she doesn't acknowledge him, but as soon as he leans conspiratorially toward her and drops his voice into a low whisper, he knows he's gained her attention. "Mother, I'm sure you've heard that I dismissed Miss Luvenia?"

Stella shoots a quick glare toward her son; her posture is still straight, and her face is still neutrally posed. "I did. Now, tell me why you would do such a thing. Going against my orders..." She clicks her tongue.

"At the time, I was just upset about Faramund's escape," Talin admits; it's a half-truth. Talin wasn't only upset at Faramund, but at the puppeteering hand of his mother too. He knows what he needs to say to convince his mother that he's still under her control and that he doesn't have any plans of his own hidden up his sleeve.

Stella's face softens ever-so-slightly. "I understand. What did you want to talk about? I can't remember the last time we had a conversation that didn't involve one of us getting our way in *something*."

Her honesty shocks him a bit, but he's thankful that he doesn't have to beat around the bush. He swallows and glances across the table as Ayne slides into her seat. He scoots even closer, wanting it to appear like he and Ayne are of different takes on what he's going to tell her. Stella's eyebrows raise. "I want to take Miss Luvenia back. I noticed Ayne getting antsy about the wedding. I think we should push it up just so she doesn't have time to find a way to get out of it." Even saying it hurts him—he would never stab Ayne in the back—but he knows he needs his mother to believe they're seeing eye-to-eye.

Stella's mouth pops open. "You want...?" She clears her throat, her gaze flicking momentarily to Ayne before returning to the earnest face of her son. "The end of the month then? It can coincide with our annual masquerade ball on the autumn solstice."

Talin forgot all about the masquerade ball—an attempt to bring the kingdom together to welcome the return of autumn. Most importantly, however, he'll have approximately two weeks to put everything into action. At the end of these two weeks, either he's going to have his freedom or he'll be dead. Surely, Stella won't let him live after attempting to exile her from Klymora.

"Thank you, Mother," Talin whispers, dipping his head in gratitude. He glances across the table and meets Ayne's gaze. He can't afford for his mother to catch on that they're planning this together, so he tries to convey their success with his eyes only. A hint of a smile curls her lips, and he knows that she understands.

When the main course arrives and he takes a bite of the finely roasted mutton, the only thing he tastes is a long-awaited victory.

CHAPTER THIRTEEN

The Owl

Miss Luvenia combs a hand through her hair and sighs, narrowing her eyes in disdain at the young prince. "Queen Stella demanded that I listen to you." She purses her lips and picks up the delicate porcelain teacup waiting on the table between them. She takes a small sip of the steaming tea before saying, "Please, Prince Talin, what is it that you want?" He can tell by her snippety tone that she's anything but pleased to see him again.

"I apologize for the way I acted before, Miss

73

Luvenia, but I need you to arrange my wedding." Talin's lips thin, and he clasps his hands together in his lap, leaning over the table and lowering his voice. "I thought Princess Ayne and I were on the same page, but it seems she's having doubts about us—and what it'll mean for our kingdoms. I need the wedding pushed up. Two weeks—on the same day as the Autumn Ball. My mother has already agreed to everything. She assured me you'd be willing to help, even after my...*behavior*."

Miss Luvenia swallows and sets the teacup back down on the saucer, clinking the porcelain. She bites her bottom lip, her eyes darting to the door, then back to Talin's eager expression. "Her Majesty has agreed to it, you say?"

Talin nods, leaning back in his seat. "Yes, she has. She says only *you* can plan the perfect royal wedding in such a short length of time."

Miss Luvenia blushes from the praise. "Then I suppose we shall begin..." She drops her gaze to the notebook she seems to always carry, removing a stick of charcoal from her pocket. She clears her throat and forces a polite smile. Her green eyes flit back up to Talin. "So, what shall the bride wear, Your Highness?" Talin hardly finds the forced pleasantries necessary, but he isn't going to complain when his plan is being executed so nicely.

Talin runs his palms down his pant legs, knowing he can just throw out anything since they won't *actually* be getting married. The entire ceremony will be a trap for his mother. Though Ayne will still have to wear the dress to keep up appearances... "I was thinking..." He takes the notebook and stick of charcoal from her, ignoring her squeak of surprise, and starts to sketch the outline of a dress on the blank parchment. "I know she likes dresses that allow for mobility, but also ones that are long and elegant." He slides the notebook toward Miss Luvenia and watches her as she studies the design. "What do you think?"

Miss Luvenia takes the charcoal from Talin and shortens the train. "If mobility is required, then the shorter the train, the better. Now, what color are we thinking? Traditional white?"

Talin nods. "It should shimmer too... She would like that." A soft smile curls his lips as he stares down at the sketch, just imagining Ayne's reaction when she sees the gorgeous gown.

"You must really love her," Miss Luvenia comments, watching the prince's face flush. She tilts her head as she inspects him, her green eyes twinkling as if she just uncovered a massive secret.

"With respect, Miss Luvenia," Talin chuckles, "I'm fourteen. I think it is impossible for me to be in love."

Miss Luvenia shakes her head, turning to the notebook once again. She starts making notes on the parchment surrounding the sketch; her handwriting is neat and elegant. "Age is only a number, dear prince, especially in the face of something so beautiful as love." She flips the page and smiles, this time genuinely. "Now, onto the groom. What shall you be wearing?"

Ayne rests her forearms on the stone railing, peering out at the distant port and the faraway land of her kingdom. Talin stops in the shadows, a step away from the moonlight that dapples through the trees. He watches her, his heart beating in sync with his mile-a-minute thoughts. So much needs to happen in such little time. Is he ready for that? For all that will change? He smooths a hand down his dress shirt and steps into the moonlight. Ayne turns to him, a smile already gracing her features. She's wearing a silver nightgown and a matching robe that falls to her ankles. Her feet are clad in a pair of white slippers that resemble gerbils, with long fluffy tails that stick out from the heels.

"Talin...how did it go?" She moves just so that her long black hair sways and reveals a small ball of white fluff sitting on the railing beside her.

It's been a little over a week since Ayne's unexpected arrival, and in between scheming the removal of Queen Stella and planning for the future with Talin, she's moved all her belongings from her palace in Gaia to her chambers here in Klymora.

Talin can't help but break into a smile. "Miss Luvenia is putting everything together, and as far as I can tell, my mother is none the wiser about our plans." He steps up beside her and rests his forearms on the railing as well. His arm touches hers and he glances away.

He watches the silent city of Caledonia. The port is deserted at this time of night, but a few lanterns on fishing boats still flicker. It was months ago that Talin declared he would marry Ayne, right there in front of the trees bordering the port, where his mother and Cedric Hemmingway decided to dash their plans of escape. And now, they've partnered together to take over Klymora and place Talin on the throne. He chuckles, earning a questioning look from Ayne.

"What's so funny?" Ayne demands, raising an eyebrow.

Talin shakes his head, listening to the sound of cicadas humming in the distance and an owl hooting from the tree nearby. He blinks in surprise and squints his eyes into the darkness, trying to locate his snow-white friend among the branches. Finally, he can make out two bright yellow eyes peering back at him. The owl hoots again, but this time its bright yellow eyes lower to lock on the shivering body of Caz.

Talin registers what's happening *too* late. As the owl's feathers catch the moonlight and its talons extend to clamp around the pulsating body of little Caz, an undignified shout parts his lips and he leaps forward to grab the owl. Though a human is no match against a winged hunter.

Within seconds, Caz is clutched in the vicious grip of the owl Talin thought was his friend. Ayne staggers and falls against the railing. Her skin pales, and her eyes widen. Talin takes her silence for shock.

A chilly late-summer breeze drifts over his skin, raising goosebumps in its wake. He stares out at the night that seemed so innocent moments before. Then, as if his brain finally starts working in sync with his muscles, he climbs up onto the railing and spots the owl hunkered back down on a tree branch, its new snack now clamped in its beak.

"Talin! What are you doing?" Ayne grabs Talin's sleeve and attempts to pull him back down, but he's not going to give up on the little gerbil so quickly. He knows how much Ayne loves Caz and how devastated she would be to lose him.

"It's going to be okay, Ayne!" he insists, ignoring the thoughts that keep bubbling to the surface of his mind: *it's too late... He can't save Caz. Why does Ayne look so calm and concentrated?* He studies the distance between the tree branch and the railing, then swallows down his fear and jumps. His palms tear against the rough bark, but he's not going to let the owl eat poor Caz, not if he can save him. Talin pulls himself up onto the branch, his hands burning with pain and covered with bloody scrapes.

He almost loses his balance, but he manages to make it to the thicker part of the branch, where he can squat down and dig his nails into the bark to keep himself rooted. The cold breeze starts to pick up, pulling at his hair and threatening to topple him over the edge of the branch and onto the ground beneath. The owl swivels its head to acknowledge the human now hunting *it*, then it shakes its wings and prepares to take off into the sky, its meal still wiggling with fear, clamped in its beak. But before the owl manages to evade capture, Talin lunges from the branch and tackles it, determination fueling his actions.

Wind dances around them as Talin and the owl spiral toward the ground. Briefly, when he glances up toward the railing and spots Ayne, he can just make out a purple haze surrounding her still form.

Death. He knew it would come. He just never imagined it'd be so...painless. He feels light as if he's flying. Could death really be so...easy? He doesn't know how long he's suspended in this limbo, unable to do anything. Finally, after several attempts, he opens his eyes, expecting to see nothing but white mist—or whatever you're supposed to see when you die. Maybe you're just supposed to see blackness. Maybe…you *can't* even see. But he *can* see right now… And what he sees is Scota; the goddess, beautiful and ethereal, staring down at him with dark brown, golden-flecked eyes. She's saying something. Tendrils of purple light leak from her fingertips and curl around her petite figure. He can't hear her. He goes to reach a hand toward her, to stroke Scota's cheek which looks so soft…but something wiggles in his grip, and suddenly his head is filled with noise, *so much* noise… Squeaking, cicadas, and Ayne's voice.

"Talin, are you okay?" Her eyebrows are knit together as she pries the owl from Talin's arms and scoops a too-still Caz into her hand. Tears pearl at her waterlines as she stares down at the rodent cupped in her palm, and then she shoots a glare toward the owl that's cowering on the ground.

Finally, everything comes into focus. Talin shakes his head. He still feels like he's falling. And the owl…why does it look like it's below him? "Ayne…" How did she get down to him so fast? He shakes his head again, more vigorously this time since he can still see purple light surrounding his friend. He pinches his eyes closed, but when he opens them, the light is still there… It's flowing from her fingertips, highlighting the grass she's standing on and leaking up toward him, enveloping him. "What the—" A scream leaves his lips and now he actually *is* falling. He thuds onto the ground that must've been a foot or two below him, making the bruises from his training session ache. Ayne's covering an ear with one hand while still cupping Caz close to her chest.

"Stop that!" she hisses, turning her fiery glare to him. "Are you trying to wake the whole kingdom?"

"I must've been hallucinating... I must've hit my head..." Talin sits up, probing for a sore spot on his head—somewhere he must've struck it when he fell from the branch. But his head isn't sore. He doesn't hurt anywhere except for the bruises he received from Ayne earlier. "Maybe I'm crazy. Maybe I'm losing my eyesight." He stares up at Ayne, trying to find any trace of the purple light that surrounded her mere moments ago. But it's gone as if it was never there to begin with. "Yep. I'm crazy. I've lost it. And just when we were going to overthrow my mother. No one is going to willingly coronate me, not if I'm seeing things. Maybe there's an elixir I can drink that'll magically make me sane again? Maybe the owl bit me and I'm suffering from some kind of owl-bite-disease." He takes a large gulp of air, unaware that he's rambling.

"Shut up, Talin," Ayne huffs, rolling her eyes. She turns toward the moon and kneels in the grass, placing Caz on her lap. Moonlight turns his fur silver and makes Ayne look like a goddess.

"Was I too late?" Talin crawls toward her. He kneels beside Ayne, biting his cheek in worry. If Caz dies—it'll be his fault. He should've warned Ayne about the owl taking residence in that tree. He should have reacted faster. He should have tackled the owl when he first realized its devious plan. He glances back at the tree, scanning to make sure the owl is long gone. But, much to his surprise, it's not. The snowy owl is nestled against the base of the tree, and the feathers of its left wing are mangled. Talin grimaces. He must've accidentally broken the owl's wing during their collision. He turns his attention back to Ayne and Caz, knowing that he needs to worry about the tiny gerbil before he worries about the offending bird.

Ayne's lips thin into a line, and her eyebrows knit together in concentration. She sniffles, grits her teeth, and turns to look at Talin. "Do you have any lemons?"

He raises an eyebrow, completely taken off guard by her question. "Lemons?"

"Yes," she says. Her eyes are slightly unfocused as if she's lost in her thoughts. "She used lemons. I think it'll work."

"I don't think we have any lemons..." He watches her deflate. "I could check the kitchen though, just in case we might have some."

"No... That's okay. This will have to work." She gently scoops Caz up and lifts his still, unmoving body toward her face.

"Ayne..." Talin reaches for her shoulder, wanting to somehow take her grief away. Caz is too still... He knows what it means, and he knows how much the small rodent means to Ayne. But he stops right before touching her because Ayne does something completely unexpected. She closes her eyes as purple light coils from her fingertips and surrounds Caz. Ayne's mouth forms an oblong 'o' and she exhales even more purple light onto the gerbil. Then, just when Talin really starts to believe he's dreaming again, Caz moves. His fluffy tail thumps against her palm, and Ayne lets out a quick laugh full of relief.

Talin's only coherent thought is: *what in Scota?*

"I should've never doubted her!" Ayne exclaims, nuzzling her nose against Caz. Tears drip down her cheeks, and her eyes crease with happiness. "I'll never doubt her again. I love you so much, little guy."

Talin's mouth falls open in shock. He doesn't know what to do—what to even think. What... just...*happened*?

Ayne, after giving Caz a thorough examination, tucks him safely on her shoulder and drapes her long hair over him to hide him from any more nighttime predators. Then she finally turns to Talin, a sheepish smile twisting her lips. "I've been meaning to tell you..."

Talin opens his mouth to say something, but he can't find the right words, so he closes it. He blinks twice, then swallows, half tempted to scream again —though waking his mother and the rest of the residents of the palace doesn't seem like the quickest way to get answers.

"Talin... I've wanted to tell you since I found out, but with everything going on, and Estanova's demand that I keep it to myself—which I didn't *really* listen to, honestly—I just, well..." She takes a steadying breath before fixing her dark, golden-flecked eyes on Talin. "I need you not to say anything until I'm done explaining. I just need you to listen." She bites her lip, her expression turning coy, before quietly saying, "Talin, I'm a witch."

CHAPTER FOURTEEN

Her Confession

Q uestions. That's all that's floating through Talin's head. *Endless questions.*

He can't believe the words that are leaving his lips as he says, "You're a...*witch*?" All his life, he's heard tales of witchcraft. Of Estanova Macellen, the first princess of his bloodline who supposedly dealt in witchcraft. Though he's never believed it. Witches and magic aren't real... They *can't* be. He lives in a world of logic and order. At least...he thought he did. His head pounds as he stares at the gerbil perched on Ayne's shoulder and at the thin veil of purple light that twirls around her fingers. If witches and magic aren't real...then how can he explain Caz miraculously surviving an owl attack and the glowing light coming from Ayne?

"H-how?" His mouth feels like it's full of sand. He shakes his head and frowns. *How is any of this real?*

"Just listen. I'll explain everything," Ayne promises, placing her hand on top of Talin's. The purple light is warm as it touches his skin. He's tempted to yank his hand away, but Ayne's touch is too lovely to willingly lose, and he doesn't want to hurt her feelings. He's not *scared*... Not really.

Ayne holds his curious gaze and smiles shyly. "Do you remember that time you took me down to the portrait room? When we first met?" She eagerly waits for him to nod. "After seeing Estanova's portrait...I started seeing her everywhere. She'd appear and disappear. She'd talk to me and tell me about her life." Ayne's voice drifts away when her eyes snag on the sprawling desert kingdom across the Abhainn River. Her smile falters. "Estanova told me about how she was in love with the first king of Gaia and how he didn't care about her magic, but her father demanded that she keep it a secret and stop whatever affair was happening with the enemy king. So, right before she stepped off the cliff in front of our elm tree, she cursed our kingdoms.

"She prophesied that she'd come back as a sixth-generation Gaian princess and fall in love with the Klymorian prince." Her eyes flick over to Talin, and a blush creeps up her cheeks. "And once they fight against everyone and everything trying to keep them apart—once they marry—then the war and conflict between the kingdoms will be stopped forever. Gaia and Klymora will unite." Her expression turns solemn. "The curse must've been twisted by those who wanted the war to continue, and that's why we've only ever heard the version where we're supposed to be kept apart lest we doom our kingdoms."

Talin follows her gaze toward her homeland, trying to grasp the entirety of what she's saying—and what he has seen. "Let me get this clear... You're telling me that you're a witch...and a reincarnation of my distant relative?" He raises an eyebrow, his mouth suddenly turning sour. If she's his relative and *not* his relative at the *same time*... how should that affect his feelings? He frowns, shaking his head in earnest. "That's *impossible*."

"Talin, I need you to understand," Ayne says calmly, bringing his hand to her lap. "I didn't think any of this was possible until I followed Faramund and ended up in your kingdom." She attempts to smile reassuringly, but her eyes reflect how tentative and unsure she's feeling. "This doesn't change anything, Talin. I'm still *me*."

He casts his gaze toward the grass, outlined and highlighted by the silvery moon. How can she say this doesn't change anything? She just took Talin's entire life, all his beliefs, and flipped it upside down. This changes *everything*.

He looks up at the starry sky. Every moment he's shared with Ayne flashes through his mind. He knew she was hiding something, but he never suspected it would be something of this magnitude.

His frown deepens, and without looking at Ayne, he quietly asks, "Can you please give me some time to myself? I'll see you tomorrow afternoon, after our fitting." He hates how cold and distant his voice sounds. He's never sounded like that while talking to Ayne.

Ayne doesn't do anything for a moment. Then she slowly stands and dusts off her dress. He gets the

90

impression that she's going to say something, but she must change her mind because she turns and walks back toward the palace without so much as a *goodnight*.

Talin listens to the hum of the cicadas, the music of the frogs and insects in the underbrush, and the quiet scratching of something behind him. He startles, remembering the injured owl.

He stands up and walks over to the tree. He tentatively kneels in front of the owl at the base of the tree. The owl's large yellow eyes glare at him in reproach, blaming Talin for the entire ordeal the owl's stuck in.

"Look. I didn't want it to go that way, but you tried to eat a friend of mine. That's not good," Talin tries to explain to the owl. Its feathers reflect the moonlight, glowing silver like the stars. He narrows his eyes at the owl's oddly bent wing, wincing. "That looks painful, little guy." Somehow, the owl's eyes narrow in spite, appearing incredibly offended as if it understands the Common tongue. Talin laughs meekly. "Okay... Let me try again. Will you allow me to help you, *beautiful girl?*" The owl's eyes brighten, and instead of cowering away from Talin's hands, she leans into his warm palms and allows him to scoop her up and hold her against his chest. "You can stay with me until your wing is better. It's the least I can do since it was my fault."

He looks around at the night one last time before escaping toward the servants' entrance and creeping into the sleeping palace. He stops in front of the doorway to the kitchen, peering farther down the hall to make sure no one is coming before pushing the door open and sneaking inside.

The ice chest is pushed against the far wall. He sneaks over and lifts the lid. There's leftover mutton from their dinner, so he tears off a piece and offers it to the owl. "It's not what you're used to," he murmurs to the owl, "but I hope it can tide you over for tonight. I'll try to find you something you are more accustomed to tomorrow." The owl blinks at him, then shifts her platter-sized eyes to the chunk of mutton, which seems to pique her interest. "For now, let's see if we can get back upstairs to my chambers unnoticed."

He silently opens the kitchen door and continues down the servants' hall until he breaks into the main corridor. His head whips to the left and right, searching for eyes spying in the darkness, or any flickering torchlight. When the coast is clear, he turns to his left and hurries toward the staircase that'll take him up to the floor that his chambers are on.

He carefully paces his steps, attempting to be as quiet as possible. On the fifth step, when his mind starts to replay the events of the night—how it turned from their usual banter to a hurricane of unsettling revelations—he catches a shadow darting across the hallway below.

He stops, peering over the railing and into the shadows edging along the wall, where he was only moments ago.

Who—or what—is lurking down there?

He can feel someone's eyes on him. The hair on the back of his neck stands on end, sensing a predator nearby. He's scared to move, just in the off-chance that the intruder hasn't seen him yet.

Then he catches a glint of light when something extends out of the shadows and into the moonlight gliding through the windows. Talin's not sure if the intruder purposefully exposed his location, or if he was trying to get closer and accidentally let the object in his hand catch the light. But Talin's heart stutters at the recognizable shape of a dagger.

Suddenly thrust out of his paralyzed state, he

darts up the steps, losing any care he had for being quiet. He won't die in silence. If he's to be murdered tonight, the entire palace will know it. He glances down at the bundle of feathers in his arms. The owl tilts her head in question, but all Talin can risk doing right now is just shaking his head.

Blood is pounding in his ears. He doesn't know if Faramund is following him or not. He's not going to wait and find out, so he throws open his door and slips inside, releasing a sigh of relief as soon as he takes his key and locks the door. He pulls his desk, chair, and weapons chest over to his door to block it. Then he settles on the edge of his bed, carefully cradling the owl, and staring blankly at the door, trying to understand the events that unfolded in mere hours.

His head starts to throb with an oncoming headache. After sitting, staring at the door for nearly an hour, he finally relents and stands up, bringing the owl over to the other side of his bed and settling her gently on the second pillow. She watches him with wide, unblinking eyes. The light coming from the open window makes her feathers sparkle. Talin studies her in awe. "If you're going to continue to reside with me, I'll have to call you something." He bites his bottom lip, tilting his head to one side. The owl mimics him playfully. "Starlight. I'll call you Starlight. You're just as beautiful and vibrant as a star itself, so it's quite fitting." He smiles when Starlight seems to nod approvingly; a beautiful name for a beautiful girl.

Talin trudges over to his side of the bed, watching the door out of the corner of his eye warily. He changes quickly into his night clothes before sliding under the sheets. He tries to push the thought of Faramund racing from the shadows to slide a dagger into his heart from his mind. He's safe. No one can get through his impenetrable barricade. If he closes his eyes now…he'll be sure to open them tomorrow.

CHAPTER FIFTEEN

The Seamstress

You're quite thin," Miss Luvenia chastises, clicking her tongue. She slides the measuring tape lower on Ayne's hips before shaking her head and clicking her tongue again. "Are you not fed?"

Ayne casts a disdainful look at Talin, who's laden with silky fabrics that'll eventually form his suit. Charcoal marks the milk-white fabric in places that need to be trimmed and tweaked. He gives her a tight-lipped smile as an apology. It's not like they have a choice of who will prepare them for their wedding, and prepare the wedding itself. Miss Luvenia is his mother's choice and the only one who would do it on such short notice since Talin brought the date forward. There's less than two weeks before their fake wedding. Talin and Ayne surmised a plan to dethrone his vicious mother, Queen Stella. Miss Dendlewind, a friend of theirs, has already carried through with her part of the operation. She's spread tales through the palace, Caledonia, and the close cities. By now, the trust in Klymora's current queen should be nearly abolished. Abhorrent scandals leeching onto her name and destroying her reputation.

Talin has a meeting with his court before dinner this evening, where he will formally request their assistance to dethrone his mother and, in turn, coronate him.

The dethroning of a monarch has rarely been done in Klymora's history. Usually, the king or queen either dies and the next in line takes their place, or the immediate heir or heiress is crowned upon their eighteenth birthday.

To dethrone a Klymorian monarch before the heir turns eighteen, every noble in the ruling court must agree, and there must be a blood heir to take the throne soon after.

If all goes to plan, the court will interrupt the wedding—where his mother will be, with no opportunity to escape, surrounded by witnesses—and strip her of her royal title and the power that goes with it.

As for Faramund... Talin gulps, turning away from Ayne so she can't catch a glimpse of the concern on his face. Faramund, after his mother is exiled, shouldn't be difficult to catch. Clearly, for some sickly reason, he's devoted to Stella. After she's gone, what would he have left? What reason would he have to stay in Caledonia? Would he still try to assassinate Talin?

Miss Luvenia's ramblings bring Talin out of his thoughts. He shakes his head, running a sweaty palm down the unstitched sleeve of his soon-to-be suit, avoiding pricking himself on a pin. He's wearing a thin white dress shirt underneath and a pair of gray trousers he doesn't care much for. Ayne's wearing a simple, ankle-length, baby blue dress with quarter-length sleeves. Miss Luvenia wanted them to wear clothes she could easily pattern over to speed up the creation of their outfits since the wedding is so soon.

Talin returns to his thoughts: *his plans will have to work.*

But...if for some Scota-forsaken reason that they don't... What will he and Ayne do?

"Looks like you're all done, Your Highness," Miss Luvenia exclaims, stepping in a circle around Ayne to study the way the shimmery white fabric falls. "Now, this is all you can see until the day of the wedding, Prince Talin. You know you should never see the bride in her gown until the big day." She casts a furtive glance his way before sliding the fabric gracefully off of Ayne, leaving her to stand in her simple, blue dress.

She blushes a bit when she catches Talin looking. She normally doesn't wear such plain outfits.

"I was told I couldn't wear anything extravagant for this. Something thin, practically invisible," she hisses, rolling her eyes in a very un-princess-like fashion which makes Talin's heart flutter even faster. Ayne definitely has a fiery temper.

"Well, if it makes you feel better. You'd look good wearing burlap." He flushes wildly after realizing that the words *actually* left his mouth, instead of staying locked away in his head.

Ayne's face turns the color of a rose. Her mouth

opens and closes as if she's struggling to find something to say. Eventually, she crosses her arms and backs toward the door, explaining how she's going to go to her chambers to get changed. But she'll be back.

After the door has long since shut, Miss Luvenia taps her foot impatiently. "You're having me work overtime to get this wedding ready in a fraction of the time it should take. Please, Your Highness, can I finish taking the measurements for your suit?"

Talin's gaze breaks away from the floor, where it was perpetually locked in embarrassment. He steps onto the stool that Ayne was just standing on and waits patiently while Miss Luvenia measures his legs and starts to pin the fabric. He watches the sky outside the window; it's a beautiful blue, bright from the sun, and perfect for the end of summer.

Miss Luvenia stands back, walks a circle around him, and then carefully and methodically removes the fabric from his body, laying it carefully on the table. "These should be done by the end of the week. The decorations for the ceremony are being gathered, harvested, and made as we speak. I'm sure your mother, the queen, will be happy to hear how everything is coming along." She directs her sharp gaze at Talin. "And how hard I've been working."

Talin picks up on her not-so-subtle, veiled implication: a raise in pay. Well, *of course,* that's what she wants.

Talin steps off the stool, feeling oddly undressed in the thin, unprincely trousers and dress shirt he was told to wear. He would usually be wearing a tailcoat or jacket over it. He dips his head in acknowledgment. "I'll pass along the message, Miss Luvenia. Now, I shall let you continue with your work. Thank you for preparing everything for our wedding. I'm sure it'll be quite memorable."

Miss Luvenia casts her cold stare upon him as he hurriedly exits the chamber.

CHAPTER SIXTEEN

The Council

Why have you summoned us, Prince Talin?" Cedric Hemmingway asks, crossing his arms and shooting a glare in Ayne's direction. "And why is *she* here? She doesn't have anything to do with this court, not after running off to do *who-knows-what* in Zhongguo of all places."

Talin melds his face into a calm mask. He's tired of Cedric acting like his superior, asking all these questions and expecting to get a response. Some things he doesn't need to know, and he'll just have to get used to that. Talin stands up from the head of the long dining table. The torches along the walls and the candles on the chandelier above him paint the room with a soft golden glow. He catches Ayne looking at him, one eyebrow raised, waiting to hear what he'll say. He runs a hand down the front of his white suit—the one he usually wears during court meetings to broadcast his status. "Cedric. Princess Ayne is my fiancée. She has as much right to be here as I do. Now, sit down and listen to what I have to say." His voice is hard and final, leaving no room for argument.

Cedric bites his lip, rebellion brewing in his eyes. But he obeys anyway, sitting down and ducking his chin, avoiding the snickers and glances of his peers.

"I have a very important reason for calling all of you here this late." He pauses to capture their attention, and as soon as everyone's eyes are on him, he continues, "You may have heard the rumor that my mother wants me dead, and how she's in cahoots with the escaped prisoner, Faramund. I'm here to tell you that all these rumors are true. I know my mother is having an affair with my father's murderer. I've witnessed it with my own eyes. And I know she helped him escape the dungeon."

The council gasps, eyebrows raised.

Cedric pipes up, "Why would she want to *kill* you, Prince Talin?"

Just the word '*kill*' brings shivers down Talin's spine. It's terrifying knowing that he's got a target painted on his back, that a murderer is lurking in the shadows, waiting to kill him just like he killed his father.

"Because I'm a threat to her reign. Because I'm trying to put her lover behind bars. Because I'm more loved by our subjects than she is... Besides, she will be the downfall of Klymora. The list keeps growing." Talin sits back down, refusing to let everyone know how his legs start to shake at the very mention of his mother. He clears his throat, ignoring the burning in his eyes and the erratic beating of his heart. How many more discoveries and threats can he handle before his heart fails him completely?

He glances over at Ayne, picturing the purple haze that leaked from her fingertips last night. He doesn't know how he feels about that... But he can't just stop caring about her. She may be a witch, but she's still Ayne.

"What should we do about it, Prince Talin?"

another noble asks. His ginger hair shines in the candlelight.

Talin smiles, grateful that they're catching on. After all, they have to do *something*. "This needs to be kept between us. This means that if your allegiance lies with Queen Stella, you should excuse yourself now. But if your allegiance lies with me, then stay and *help* me." He's pleasantly surprised when no one stands up, not even Cedric Hemmingway. They're all watching him, faces drawn and intent. Determined to protect their prince and their future. His face warms. Now, he needs to take the risk and ask them to dethrone his mother. A practically unspeakable act.

"Princess Ayne and I have come up with a plan to secure our future and the future of everyone in Klymora…" He takes a steadying breath, wiping his sweaty palms on his pant legs under the table. "We need to dethrone my mother and coronate me before my eighteenth birthday."

Another gasp resounds about the dining hall. Faces pale and jaws drop. Cedric's mouth opens and closes. He runs a hand through his hair and leaves chunks disheveled across his forehead.

"But you're *fourteen*, Your Highness," Cedric

points out, grimacing. "We can't appoint a child to rule a kingdom. Especially not in the midst of a war."

"As far as the threats from Emperor Neo of Zhongguo go, he's drawn his focus away from us and toward Rutheria. My age won't stop me from doing my absolute best to protect Klymora and keep my subjects safe. I'm insulted that you think it would," Talin exclaims, narrowing his eyes at Cedric. "Our wedding is planned to happen on the same day as the Autumn Ball. My mother is guaranteed to be at the wedding, so that's the only time we can arrest and dethrone her in front of an influential crowd.

"The Klymorian law states that if the entire royal court is in agreement and a direct heir is alive, a Klymorian monarch can be dethroned." Talin frowns. "This will work. It has to."

"And if it doesn't?" Cedric asks, earning a slap on the shoulder by one of the nobles closest to him. He winces and glares at the offending peer.

"If it doesn't work, then my mother will still be queen, and I will be dead."

Cedric's face turns grave as if the entirety of the situation is finally settling in. They have no choice but to dethrone Queen Stella. She's too much of a risk to Prince Talin and to the country.

"Let's take a vote, shall we?" Talin stands back up, struggling to keep his hand from shaking as he lifts it into the air. "Raise your hand if you hereby grant me permission, upon the stipulations of the first Klymorian king, to dethrone Queen Stella Macellen and thereafter coronate me, Prince Talin Macellen, as king of Klymora."

Around the table, hands slowly rise into the air. Unsure and hesitant. Talin knew his age would be a problem, but he could easily have the coronation planned for his fifteenth birthday. Would it be a small comfort to them to know that their king won't be fourteen? That he'd be fifteen?

He watches the nobles' hands inch into the air, following them around the table until they get to Cedric.

Cedric looks squeamish in his seat. He knows that Prince Talin needs him to raise his hand to finalize the vote and officially set the action of dethroning Queen Stella in place... Would he stand against him? Talin knows they've had their bouts and quarrels, and that they've never really gotten along. But surely he doesn't believe that Queen

Stella is more fit to rule than Prince Talin? Especially when his life is on the line?

Cedric slowly looks up at Talin, a small reassuring smile on his face as if he has come to a conclusion. Without saying anything, he pushes back his chair, earning a squeak of surprise and confusion from his friends on the council, and stands up.

Talin's about to collapse into his seat in defeat when Cedric silently raises his hand.

Relief washes over Talin, and he sags into his chair. The hard part is done. The council has officially decided to dethrone his mother. His life... *is saved*.

Cedric nods toward Talin. "I know we've never gotten along, Your Highness. But I also know you were born to rule this country, and it would be a great act of disservice to my people if I did anything but raise my hand."

"Thank you, Lord Hemmingway." Talin locks eyes with him, an unsaid truce growing between them.

"You did it, Talin," Ayne congratulates, sheepishly grinning at him as they walk to the elm tree. He can tell that she's still unsure of his feelings about her magic. They never talked about that dramatic night, and it wouldn't do them any good to pretend like nothing happened, because *something* did happen. Something life-altering.

"Ayne..." Talin starts slowly, trying to find the right words to express what he's feeling. He's never been good at telling her his thoughts unless it's in a letter or his dreams. In person, he always gets tongue-tied and ends up making a fool out of himself. He's determined not to do that this time. "I think I'm going to need to you to tell me everything. If I'm to trust these abilities of yours, I would like to know how they work and...well, *why*." He watches his boots instead of looking at her. They remain in silence until they reach the elm tree. Ayne sidles into a grassy spot between huge, unearthed roots while Talin sits down and crosses his legs. He waits for her to say something.

Ayne purses her lips, then sighs. Her lilac purple dress bunches around her legs, and the silver embroidered flowers catch the last traces of sunlight. Her hair shimmers as well, and at first Talin thinks it's the gold threads she usually laces throughout her raven-black hair, but this time... He reaches out and rubs the silver strands between his fingers, eyebrows knitted in wonder.

"It just happened," Ayne explains, tucking it bashfully behind her ear. She blushes, and her eyes sparkle as if they're going to water. "It's a trait of being a witch. I don't know why, but parts of our hair start to gray." She looks back up at him under the canopy of her thick eyelashes. A small, humiliated smile twists her lips. "It's not very princess-like, is it?"

"I think it's beautiful," Talin says without thinking. But it's true. Her hair isn't gray...it's silver and magnificent, capturing the light. It's as if the stars are woven into her hair. A crease forms between Ayne's eyebrows, and she averts her gaze, ducking her head.

"As I mentioned before, I only discovered I'm a witch when you took me down to the portrait room and I met Estanova's ghost. I started having visions of her life. She showed me how in love she was with Dominic Edelweiss, the first king of Gaia, and that she cursed both our kingdoms because her father wouldn't allow her to be with him. She showed me a vision of her leaping off this very cliff," Ayne casts a withered look over her shoulder at the drop mere feet away. "And she told me not to tell anyone. Not unless I trusted them completely." She glances back up at Talin, guilt written across her face. "I only told my family. I had to. I couldn't keep something this huge a secret from them. And I certainly couldn't figure out what to do without them. So...they sent me to Zhongguo to apprentice under Maya Lee.

"She's the only known witch, supposedly. She taught me so much... I now have some semblance of control over my magic. She also made Caz immortal, so that's why the owl didn't kill him."

Immortal...

Immortality exists?

And ghosts?

How can all these things be real, right under his nose?

Talin frowns, but refuses to interrupt her, not when he's finally piecing together Ayne's mysterious life.

"I won't bore you with the tiny details. But a lot happened over in Zhongguo. Maya rebelled against the emperor, which caused him to hunt her down and forced us to flee. Sir Mason, my courtier, was shot with an arrow and taken as a prisoner by the emperor. Maya went back for him, resulting in her being taken as well." Ayne's bottom lip wobbles and she steadies it with her front teeth. She seems on the verge of crying. "Oh Scota, Talin... I failed them. I don't know what happened to them, or what's going to. I should've stopped the boat and gone back for them. Why didn't I? What kind of a princess am I, leaving my friends to that fate?"

Talin takes her hand, smoothing calming circles over the back of her hand with his thumb. "You knew you were needed here. That doesn't make you a bad princess," Talin whispers. His heart hurts watching Ayne crumble before him. "I'll send word to Zhongguo and ask about their well-being if that helps. That's all I can do right now."

Ayne sniffles and leans forward, collapsing against his chest. Her body heaves with her sobs. Talin wraps his arms around her, just letting her cry. Once she releases all her pent-up tears, he...*might*... let go.

"You're an amazing princess, Ayne. You've saved so many people already. I'm sure Maya and Mason will be okay." He knows it's not much in the way of reassurance, but it's all he can offer her right now. Empty promises won't do them any good.

"Talin...?" Ayne whispers, wrapping her arms around his back.

Talin pushes her hair out of her face so he can look down at her. "Yes, Ayne?"

She hiccups and shakes her head. "Why are you such a good friend to me?"

Talin chuckles, slightly taken aback by such an absurd question. "Because you're Ayne Edelweiss. You have a heart of gold, a temper of fire, and magic at your fingertips. You're enchanting, Ayne. Everywhere you go, life seems vibrant and worth all its hardships." He comes up short of breath when Miss Luvenia pops into his head. He hadn't given her remark much thought before.

'You must really love her...'

At first, he dismissed it as an impossibility because of his age. But if he can dethrone his mother and rule an entire kingdom, then surely, he can admit the feelings that have been brewing in his heart ever since he met Ayne.

One is never too young to be in love.

"Ayne?" Talin says, cautiously. He bites his cheek, trying to pluck up enough courage to finally say it. She deserves to know. But what if...what if

113

she doesn't feel the same? What if his admission makes her feel uncomfortable? What if he ruins their entire friendship by saying this?

"Talin?" She sniffles again, but her sobs have quieted. He hopes his declaration comforts her, at least a little.

He opens his mouth, prepared to say that he loves her—but shuts it. He tries again, but his heart is beating too fast. "Ayne..." He takes a long inhale, trying to steady his nerves. "You...um...smell really nice."

Ayne chuckles, a smile breaking onto her face. "Thank you, Talin. You smell really nice too."

CHAPTER SEVENTEEN

The Footsteps

T alin strokes his fingers across Starlight's back. She lets out a soft, satisfied sigh and nudges her face into the crook of his arm. The moon is high in the night sky as Talin watches over the sleeping city of Caledonia. Starlight's tree stands proudly in the dark, leaves starting to turn orange and brown. Autumn is coming, and with it, an entirely new era ruled by a defiant prince.

"Do you think I'll be a good king, Starlight?" Talin asks, smiling down at the moon-kissed owl.

Starlight nuzzles him, and he chuckles, taking that as a yes. He's nervous, knowing that everyone will be watching him, not just those in Caledonia or even Klymora. *Everyone.* The world will be watching him, studying him, judging him... He can't afford one wrong move, not *one* mistake. His lips straighten into a line, and he lifts his chin, peering out at his kingdom, determination washing over him in waves. He won't let his people down. No matter what happens, he will always put them first.

He takes a shaky breath and turns to head back to his chambers. Starlight's body turns heavy as she falls into a peaceful sleep. Her wing has been healing nicely over the past few days, but she still has a long way to go before she's able to fly again.

"Let's get you to bed," Talin whispers, smoothing a hand down her feathers. He's made a little spot for her on his windowsill so she can look out at nature and not feel so cooped up.

The palace at night is quiet. Startlingly quiet. Usually, there's the chatter of maids who think there's nobody around, the joyous laughter of the cooks drifting up from the kitchen, or even the calculated conversations of the nobles who reside on the grounds. But tonight...there's just his

116

footsteps…and…

The hair on the back of Talin's neck stands on end, and his shoulders tense. He stops walking, wondering if maybe his mind is playing tricks on him. But no, much to his terror, another pair of footsteps stops ten or so yards behind him.

He starts walking again, too terrified to glance behind him and possibly catch a peek at the person who's so *clearly following* him.

He heads straight for his chambers, trying not to jostle Starlight as she peacefully sleeps, but it's hard when the footsteps behind him start to draw near, and he shifts into a frantic sprint. He can see his door, only twenty more feet and he's at it—

A hand grabs the back of his shirt and pulls him to a stop. The blade of a dagger catches the flickering light from a dim torch mounted on the wall as it rests against his neck. He can feel the slick metal with every heartbeat.

"If you kill me before I marry Ayne, then my mother gets nothing," Talin says, trying to make his voice sound stronger than he currently feels. Unfortunately, it comes out in a meek rasp. He sucks in his bottom lip and bites it with his front two teeth. If he's going to die, he's not going to die sniveling like a coward. His father didn't die like that. His father died distinguished, known throughout the land as a great king. If he's not even going to be given the chance to rule, then he's going to go out as nothing less than a brave prince.

The voice of his assailant is deep and raspy; the cool timbre that is unique to Faramund is pushed into an undertone. Maybe Faramund is second-guessing himself... Or maybe he doesn't want to kill Talin at all. "Queen Stella has other ways to get the Edelweiss's gold, Prince Talin. You're becoming too much of a problem, shoving your nose in places it doesn't belong, insisting upon throwing me—her *lover*—in that nasty cell." He spits on the ground by Talin's feet. "You're no longer necessary. So, she instructed me to silence you—just like I silenced your father."

"How is she going to get their gold?" Talin asks, wincing as Faramund presses the blade deeper, drawing a single drop of blood that drips down his neck.

Faramund leans closer to Talin's ear, his acrid breath brushing the peach fuzz on his cheek. "That one noble on your court. The loud-mouth. What's his name? Cedar?"

"Cedric?" Talin responds, furrowing his brow. Cedric already made it known that he doesn't want Talin dead—that Talin would be a much better ruler than Stella. Would he marry Ayne and give all her possessions to Stella, knowing she is the reason Talin would be dead? Cedric Hemmingway may be a snake of a man, but he wouldn't sink that low. The muscles in Faramund's arms flex, and Talin squeaks, pinching his eyes shut in preparation for the final blow. But it doesn't come. He opens one eye at a time. "You're not going to...kill me?"

Faramund's voice is rough as if he's internally battling with himself. "I *should* kill you. That's what Queen Stella commanded me to do."

"But..." Talin squeaks, lowering his eyebrows over his eyes. Starlight blinks up at him, a pitiful squeak coming from her throat as if she knows how dire the situation is.

"But you're just a child... And I've always liked you, Talin," Faramund admits, sounding defeated. With a sigh, Faramund releases Talin, who stumbles forward, clutching Starlight to his chest. "I won't ask about the owl," Faramund decides, nodding toward the white bundle in the prince's arms. It seems that a prince carrying an injured owl through the palace at night isn't the strangest thing he's encountered.

Talin holds the assassin's eyes. With a curt nod, Talin says, "Go. Get out of my kingdom."

Faramund narrows his eyes, lifting his chin. The stubble on the side of his face is illuminated by the torchlight, and the canvas pants that hang too loose on his wirey figure cast a strange shadow across the floor. "What do you have planned, Prince Talin?"

Talin shakes his head, knowing he can't tell Faramund what's going to happen. He may not want to kill the assassin right now, but that doesn't mean he trusts Faramund. He still detests the man. "Get out of my kingdom," Talin repeats. He's only sparing the assassin's life because Faramund spared his own... At least, that's what Talin is telling himself. In reality, he doesn't want to be a murderer. He doesn't want to condemn anyone to death.

"What about Queen Stella? She loves me," Faramund says, studying Talin with his dark brown eyes.

"She doesn't love you," Talin adds slowly, softening his voice. He takes a step toward Faramund, offering him a sympathetic smile. Starlight cranes her head to look between the two.

"She doesn't even love *me,* and I'm her flesh and blood." He shakes his head. "She's using you, Faramund. Just…get out of here before she's done using you and decides you're expendable as well."

Faramund opens his mouth to say something, but Talin cuts him off again. "This is your only chance at a new life. I won't hunt you down. No one will come after you. You can simply walk away and live out the rest of your life. I suggest you take it."

Without waiting for Faramund's response, Talin turns on his heel and continues to his chambers. The hair on his spine is still standing at attention, aware that he just turned his back on his father's killer.

"Thank you," Faramund's voice is calm, quiet, and devastated at the same time. He takes a step back, then turns around and disappears down the hallway.

Talin doesn't watch him go, instead, he opens his door and slips inside. Once his door is firmly shut and locked, he collapses against it and sinks to the floor. Tears start to fall from his eyes, dripping onto his shirt and across Starlight's feathers. She nuzzles her face into his chest in an effort to comfort Talin.

Talin's chest heaves as he sobs. Crying from the fear of having a dagger held against his throat. Crying for his father, whose murderer Talin let walk away with no repercussions. And crying because he's terrified of change; of letting down his kingdom and possibly disappointing his people.

Eventually, when his tears dry, he pushes up from the floor and crosses to the window. He peers outside, watching the lanterns at the dock flicker. A familiar silhouette is standing at the dock, talking to a stocky man and a frail woman on a ferry. Talin's surprised there are still people out there since it's so late.

He sets Starlight down and makes sure she's comfortable. After checking the progress of her wing, he returns his attention to the window. Faramund takes a step on board the ferry, and the ferry master accepts a pouch of what Talin can only assume are coins. The older woman hobbles over to the cabin that's erected near the back of the raft-like ferry. Faramund looks back at the stone palace cloaked in ivy and up at the prince's window. His shoulders lower as he sighs, turning around to follow the older woman into the cabin.

A weight lifts from Talin's chest as the ferry

leaves the dock, taking Faramund and the threat of Talin's imminent demise with it.

Talin watches it float down the Abhainn River, the moonlight glinting off the water and casting the ferry in a silver glow.

Cicadas start their familiar song; the musical sound drifting up to Talin's window.

A small smile curls Talin's lips, and he turns to watch Starlight sleep, knowing that everything will be okay. That he'll be okay. At least for now.

CHAPTER EIGHTEEN

The Wedding

T alin paces back and forth in the dressing chamber. Why is he nervous, when he knows the entire day is a charade? He's not *actually* getting married. Nothing for him is changing—well, except for the fact that he'll be dethroning his mother and claiming the crown for himself.

But he's not nervous about that, not like he should be. He's nervous about seeing her... Beautiful Princess Ayne, all dressed in white. The vision alone sends goosebumps up his arms.

He stops pacing to look at himself in the mirror for the hundredth time in the past half hour. His curly, light brown hair is combed to one side. Cuffing his neck is a dainty gray bow tie, hand-selected by Miss Luvenia to match the white suit he's wearing.

White is the color for the highest-ranking nobles —*royalty*—so Miss Luvenia deemed it fit that he should wear it at his wedding.

He runs a hand down the front of his jacket, the coattails of which fall elegantly behind him and sway with his every movement. A pearl clasp brings the jacket together in the center of his chest and catches the sunlight as it falls through the window behind him, reflecting in the mirror.

He feels sort of bad about using Miss Luvenia— of wasting her time and energy for a wedding that's just a hoax. But he needed to convince his mother, and since his mother trusts Miss Luvenia, and chose her herself, it needed to be done.

Talin tucks a loose curl behind his ear and smiles sheepishly at himself. In only a few minutes, he'll be walking down the aisle to overly romanticized music and standing on a slightly raised dais beside a priest, with a couple hundred people staring straight at him. He's used to being watched, especially at court. But this is just *somehow* different.

They'll be gawking at him, wondering what's going through his head to be getting married at fourteen. But they don't understand politics—or being a pawn in Queen Stella's game.

And when everything gets flipped upside down? When Queen Stella is dethroned right in front of her subjects? That'll unleash chaos—chaos he's supposed to be able to reign in.

He takes a deep breath and wipes his sweaty palms down his pants. *He can do this*. He *has* to do this. If he doesn't, then he's going to doom his entire kingdom.

He *has* to be brave enough... *He has to be*.

There's a light knock on the door, and he almost jumps out of his skin.

A man pokes his head in, eyebrows raised. "Are you ready, Prince Talin?"

Talin gives him a curt nod, wringing his hands together. The man tracks the movement, his lips thinning into a sympathetic smile.

The man holds the door wide for Talin, and Talin stumbles forward, chanting the mantra *I-can-do-this* over and over again in his head.

But as the chatter of the people waiting in their seats for the ceremony grows louder, he starts to doubt that he *can* do this—that he even possesses the bravery necessary to pull off such a thing.

But he's been through a lot: he survived Faramund's attack. He has freed countless people from being wrongfully accused. And he's spent the past couple of weeks taking care of Starlight, the snowy owl that's safely tucked up in his chambers with a healing wing.

He's made a lifelong friend out of an entirely unexpected person. He's got the support of his court behind him, and he's destined to be a great king just like his father.

He takes another deep breath, filling his lungs. *He can do this.* And, this time, when the words echo around inside his head, he knows them to be true.

Talin steps into the great hall. Rose-tinted wooden pews line either side, filled with roughly two hundred of the palace and Caledonia's residents. Since the wedding was on such short notice, Stella decided just to have the nobles within the palace and the higher-ranking subjects of Caledonia present. Talin's sure that if they planned the wedding months and months in advance, it would be on a great sweeping hill with the entire country in attendance. He's glad it was kept small, though the segregation of lower-ranking citizens to higher-ranking nobles is unjust and unnecessary. Every citizen of Klymora is his subject, and they should all be treated as such, with no discriminatory differences because of their classes. Of course— that's what Talin's dream world would be like, but reality is very different.

A white woven rug trails down the center of the hall, all the way to the raised dais at the very end. The priest is waiting—an old man with a shiny bald scalp and a face full of wrinkles. His smile is kind as he looks up and notices Talin standing at the entrance to the hall. He's holding a leather-bound version of Scota's Scripture in his hand, and a goblet of wine sits on the small table behind him. It's custom in Klymora—and much of Gaia as well—to have the newly married couple drink from a goblet of the oldest wine in Klymora. It's said to seal the partnership and make it official in the eyes of Scota.

Talin spots his court sitting in the front row. Sunlight glides in from the mosaic windows lining either side of the great hall. Cedric turns in his seat and meets Talin's eyes, and surprisingly, he smiles.

Cedric has always been the unruliest of his court; he's always wanting to be first, and always wanting to do something that will make him gain a step up the social ladder, usually at the expense of others. But right now... He seems different. More content. Maybe even at peace—if that's not stretching it.

Talin smiles back at him, and Cedric gestures with his chin for Talin to start walking. Only then does Talin take note of the gentle music swelling through the hall. White rose petals are sprinkled across the rug, and he forces himself to start walking. All he needs to do is get to that dais, and then his part is complete for the time being. One step in front of the other. He can handle that. *One step in front of the other.*

The crowd watches him as he slowly walks down the center aisle, chin held high, and intently studying the curved architecture of the Grand Hall. If he notices how many eyes are on him, studying and judging him, then he might falter. He might trip and fall right in the middle of his fake wedding. He never feels nervous at court, even though there are just as many people, if not more. So why does he feel so nervous now? His wedding is a hoax to fool his mother—so why does he have a flurry of butterflies in his stomach and his heart pounding a symphony in his chest? Maybe because he knows what happens next: he exiles his mother and takes the crown for himself, altering not only his future— but the future of his entire kingdom.

He reaches the dais and shakily steps up, hoping no one notices how hard his hands are quivering. He turns to look at Cedric—who his mother appointed ring bearer—and raises his eyebrows. Cedric holds up the little black ring pouch and gives Talin a subtle nod before tucking it back into the pocket of his ash-gray suit. There *are* two rings inside, even though they are *not* going to rest around anyone's finger; Stella commissioned a metalsmith in Caledonia to make the pair of rings out of black tungsten, embedding a small row of three diamonds in Talin's and a very large, very shiny diamond on Ayne's.

Then Talin's eyes are tugged to the end of the hall as the music swells again, reaching a sweet crescendo before falling back. The pianist near the entrance of the hall is a feeble old woman— surprisingly, she's not retired already. Though Talin supposes that if music is what makes your heart beat, you can't just *stop* playing.

The crowd stands from their seats, all facing toward the entrance as a woman clad in a beautiful white gown appears, two small kingdom girls flanking either side of her, white wicker baskets of various flowers dangling from their tiny arms.

Talin gasps, stumbling forward a step. The priest has to reach out with his arm to make sure Talin doesn't fall off the tiny ledge of the dais.

Gorgeous.

Breathtaking.

Enchanting...

None of these words do her justice.

Ayne.

His Ayne.

The pearl-white gown falls in elegant waves, exposing her tan shoulders to be kissed by the afternoon light. A dainty silver necklace rests between her collarbones, and he has to squint to realize that it's a tiny sun. The gown falls in soft, angelic waves around her feet. Her face is left untouched, save for the iridescent shimmer that highlights her cheekbones and her eyelids. When she glances up at him, her full lips part as a small gasp escapes her, and he nearly tumbles off the dais again.

He doesn't seem fit for a crown, not when Ayne is standing before him like Scota herself. Ayne was born to be a queen. It would be impossible to picture her as anything else.

Ayne steps up on the dais as the flower girls twirl about, tossing the last remnants of the flower petals at the crowd before finding their respective seats next to their parents. She smiles at him, which sends a jolt through his entire body.

The priest clears his throat before ordering everyone to sit down. Talin steals a glance at his mother, who's situated smack-dab in the middle of the first row. Her legs are crossed under the midnight-blue silk gown she chose to wear, and her eyes are outlined with black kohl. She looks bored as if she can't wait for this entire thing to be over. Probably so she can step in and snatch everything that should rightfully be Ayne's.

Ayne and Talin exchange a look before peering over at the court to their right. Cedric takes the hint, standing up from his seat and garnering the attention of everyone in the Grand Hall.

Slowly, Talin's court crosses the aisle to stand in front of the queen. Their faces are grim, and their posture is regal. Cedric pulls out the scroll he carefully situated in the inside pocket of his jacket, opposite the ring pouch, and unrolls it in front of the queen. She cocks her head, lip curling as a venomous demand springs to life on her tongue.

"What in the name of Scota do you *think* you're doing?" she barks, snarling at the assembled court. She stands up, towering over Cedric. But he doesn't shrink under her stare; he doesn't even quiver. "You're interrupting the ceremony. Sit down. *Now*." Her eyes darken like a predator sizing up her prey.

"Queen Stella Macellen of Klymora, we're dethroning you under the allegations of coerced murder and attempted murder. Under the ruling of the first king of Klymora, we have the right—as a united court—to force you from the throne and to pass the monarchy to your only son, Prince Talin Macellen. Under Klymorian law and the goddess Scota, we banish you from this kingdom. You, Stella Macellen, are hereby removed from the throne and exiled from the country of Klymora." Cedric rolls the scroll back up and tucks it in his pocket. His face is flushed from the action of delivering such a life-altering verdict, but he holds his chin high as Stella glares down at him, eyes wide and mouth agape with shock.

"You can't—" she squawks, stepping away from the two nobles who are trying to bind her wrists together. She holds her hands up in an attempt to prevent them from succeeding.

"It is a unanimous decision that upholds the laws of the kingdom. There is no getting out of this, Stella," Cedric says quietly, each word a blow that makes Stella gasp with outrage. But even she can't see a loophole in the centuries-old ruling.

Finally, after countless minutes of struggling, the nobles secure the rope tightly around Stella's wrists, binding them behind her. Her skin is ashen, and her eyes are glazed. When the court and their prisoner turn to walk down the center aisle, the entire crowd is gawking at them, then at Talin. Jaws have fallen open, and eyes are bulging from people's heads. The entire hall has fallen into a stupor of shocked silence.

"Do we continue—" the priest starts, holding the book of Scota's Scripture aloft in his hand.

Ayne smiles kindly at him before reaching across the space between them and taking Talin's hand. Sweetly, she says, "No. That won't be necessary." She turns to look at the crowd, her cheeks tinged with the lightest pink, as she shouts over the somehow suffocating silence, "We will see you all tonight for the Autumn Ball! Please, do enjoy the festivities and food supplied at the reception!" Then she tugs on Talin's hand and starts back down the center aisle, a blissful song escaping between her lips.

She hurries down the corridor and pushes open the doors to the back garden, stepping outside as the autumn chill nips at her exposed shoulders. Her black hair is wavy with gold threads spread throughout, and cupping the sides of her ears are silver cuffs with beautiful pearl beads.

"We're free," Ayne trills, throwing her hands up in the air and beaming at the autumn sun.

Talin watches her, his heart thundering in his ears. She's never been so stunning before. So happy and thrilled with life. He steps forward, bucking up enough courage to extend his pinky finger toward her. She glances down at it with confusion written across her face. "I have to say something, Ayne, and I don't want it to change anything between us. I just have to say it or I might die."

The tone of his voice catches her off guard, and

she pulls her lips to the side, furrowing her brow. But she trusts him, so she links her pinky with his and says, "You can tell me anything, and I promise it won't change anything between us."

Talin bites his lip, his breathing turning slightly labored. But he needs to say it. He can't hold it in any longer. If he does, he might implode.

She deserves to know.

"Ayne... Beautiful Ayne..." He swallows, stepping toward her. Her cheeks flush, and she glances down at his lips.

"Talin?"

Talin clenches his hands into fists at his sides. "I love you, Ayne. You are my sun. My light. You dispel all my worries, my fears, and all the darkness in my life." He takes another tiny step toward her. "I love you with the entirety of my soul. *I love you.*"

She blinks up at him in surprise. But then tears glisten in her eyes, and she's grinning—not exactly the response Talin was expecting. He was expecting to be punched once or twice, pushed, or given the silent treatment for the remainder of the week. But her...glowing like this? Overflowing with happiness and joy? He couldn't ask for anything better—

Ayne's lips crash into his, and he stumbles backward, taken off balance. She steps away just as fast, her entire body shifting from tan to rose.

"What just—"

"I love you too, Talin," Ayne says, shaking her head as twin tears crest her cheeks. She bites her bottom lip, her smile growing wider by the second. She links her hand with his and pulls him toward their special spot. "Let's watch the river while everyone else is getting ready for the ball."

"You don't want to change for the masquerade?" Talin raises his eyebrows.

Ayne shakes her head, a bell-like laugh leaving her throat. "I don't need a mask since I have no reason to hide."

CHAPTER NINETEEN

The Masquerade

When they enter the Eastern Ballroom, the Autumn Ball to welcome the new season is already in full swing. Ayne's radiant, smiling at the timid faces of the people around her. Everyone is glancing at the pair as they stride to the center of the dance floor. Talin would much rather hide near the banquet table and eat, avoiding the prying eyes of his court, but Ayne insists on dancing. So, with a shrug, he clasps one hand around her waist and the other in her hand, offering her a slightly timid, coy smile. He can still feel her phantom lips against his, the puff of her warm breath mingling with his own. His heart rate increases, and he blushes. He doesn't know what he did to deserve to hold the sun in his arms, but Scota is he *blessed*.

The quartet situated on a dais against the far wall starts to increase in tempo, thrusting their horsehair bows across the gentle strings of their violins and cellos. The music swells, increasing the pace of the dancers, before settling into a slow song. Ayne rests her cheek against Talin's chest, and he hopes she can't hear how frantically his heart is beating. Though, by her quiet, content chuckle, he assumes she does.

He rests his face against the top of her head, taking note that she smells like flowers. Right now, at this moment, everything feels perfect. But he knows that as soon as the ball ends and he steps into the corridor, he will have to acknowledge that his former life is over. That in mere months, he will be king.

King of a confused, devastated country. A child king without parents to lead him. He swallows the knot in his throat formed by the thought of his mother leaving for an unfamiliar country. He knows she deserves it for what she did to his father...but she's the only family he has left. And now...he's alone.

Orphaned.

"It will be okay, Talin," Ayne murmurs against his chest. Her eyes are closed, revealing a light dusting of white sparkles across her eyelids. She nuzzles her cheek against him like he's a comfortable pillow. "You're going to be an amazing king, Talin. Even better than your father."

After shaking himself from his stupor, he runs his fingers through her hair, ignoring the fact that he's messing it up. He hugs her to him, needing to hold someone and be held in return. Right now...he doesn't *want* to be alone. He wants to be with *her*. He wants to look down and see those perfect eyes shimmering with golden flecks. Ayne snakes her hands around his back, hugging him with the same ferocity as he's hugging her. "Ayne?"

"Yes, Talin?"

"Thank you," he whispers, lacing the words with the intensity of his feelings; his gratitude and friendship.

She glances up at him, one eyebrow arced over her dazzling brown eyes. "For what, Talin?"

140

Talin's lips twist up in a sheepish, earnest smile. When he looks at her, he feels complete. As if he had a hole in his heart his entire life, and only now does it feel full. "For being my friend. My best friend. For adding light back into my life."

Ayne blinks, looking awestruck by his admission. Then she beams as bright as the golden sun. "You're too sweet, Talin." Her eyes turn into crescents as her smile widens. The light from the chandeliers makes her tan skin radiant and the powder across her eyelids sparkle. "Thank you for being my best friend too. I know for a fact that I wouldn't be where I am today if it wasn't for you."

"Is it because I kidnapped you?" Talin jeers.

Ayne laughs, shaking her head. "No, you silly. Well—I guess technically." She bites her lip and then shrugs. A thoughtful look passes over her face. "Because you helped me...discover who I want to be. *How* I want to be." She furrows her brow as if something dawns on her.

"What is it, Ayne?" Talin asks, giving her a quizzical look.

Her eyes widen, and she waves his question away. "Oh. Nothing. I just realized something."

"And what's that?"

The music swells, dancing over their skin as the musicians' speed increases, drawing their bows over their strings and plucking feverishly on their cellos.

Ayne seems to fall back into her thoughts before abruptly stepping away from him. He frowns. Did he do something wrong? Did he say something wrong?

Ayne looks conflicted. "I have to go."

"Go?" Talin asks, confused, and admittedly, hurt. Is she running away from him? Does she regret what she said? What did he do... What did he do to make her run away? "Why?" He winces when his voice comes out croaked.

Ayne steps back toward him, pressing her palm to his chest. "It has nothing to do with you, Talin. I just had a personal revelation. I need to see my family immediately."

"There are no ferries to Gaia at night," Talin explains, wondering why she needs to see her family so urgently. What kind of personal revelation did she have? And if it's not about him, then what is it? He wonders if he'll ever know.

"I'll wait until morning. But right now, I need to be by myself. I need to think. You understand." Her hand slips from his chest, and he immediately notes

142

the absence of her touch.

He's not sure if he *does* understand...but if that is what Ayne wants, then he's not going to stop her. "Of course," he mutters, pressing his lips into a line when she gives him one last sympathetic look before turning to head back through the doors of the Eastern Ballroom. He feels all eyes on him, but when he finally snaps his gaze away from her, he realizes that no one is even paying attention. Not anymore. They're immersing themselves in conversation, dancing, and eating at the long tables lining the sides of the ballroom. He's standing in the middle of the dance floor, completely forgotten and longing for the one person who doesn't want him. Well...not right now. Right now, she wants to be alone.

He sighs and heads toward the doors, admiring the intricate swirls and flowers engraved in the polished wood frame. He doesn't notice the noble make his way through the crowd to stop in front of him until Talin almost runs into him. He diverts his attention from the intricate details of the room to the man. "Lord Hemmingway? Is something the matter?"

Cedric smiles breezily, but something flashes in

his eyes. "Listen, Prince Talin..."

His tone of voice catches Talin off guard, piquing his curiosity.

Cedric's smile turns empathetic. "I can only imagine how hard it must be...to send your mother away and take the throne at such a young age. But..." His cheeks tinge pink, and he seems to choke on his words, forcing them out with a deep exhale. "I'm thankful that you're going to be our king. I truly believe that with you leading Klymora, we can finally do some actual good..." He shakes his head in an attempt to shake away his embarrassment. "I just had to say that."

Talin's lost for words. He's never liked Cedric, finding him too egotistical and rudely vulgar, so hearing the exact words he was longing for come from him sends his brain spiraling into confusion. His tongue sticks to the roof of his mouth as he tries to form words. With a gulp and a slightly nervous chuckle, Talin finally says, "Thank you, Lord Hemmingway. You have no idea how much hearing that means to me."

"I also thought you should know that your mother is going to be kept in the dungeon while we finish the rest of the paperwork and arrange transport for her to leave Klymora. If I were you, I would stay clear of her after everything that happened today," Cedric says, giving him a nod before disappearing into the throng of dancers. Talin takes a steadying breath, wondering if he can do it. If he can be a successful king. He gives the room a last glance, relaxing as gentle laughter and content smiles flit around the room.

He tucks his hands behind him and heads out the doors and down the hallway, listening to the gentle pitter-pattering of rain on the ground outside.

Right now, all he wants to do is check on Starlight and see how her wing is healing. He wants to return her to nature as soon as she's ready. He doesn't like the thought of forcing her to be so still, away from the moonlight that shines on her snow-white feathers and the fresh air that envelopes her.

CHAPTER TWENTY

The Letter

Talin falls asleep, stroking Starlight's feathers. She sleeps soundly in his arms as the sun rises in the sky. He wakes up, his neck and back stiff from falling asleep situated on the windowsill. The sun is golden, high in the slightly cloudy sky. It reflects off the Abhainn River, highlighting the ferries that rest at the port. He jolts forward and startles Starlight from her slumber. The events of last night flood to the forefront of his mind, and he gently sets Starlight down, analyzing her wing thoroughly before sleepily stumbling from his room. He wants to catch Ayne before she leaves—but he seems to have slept in, which means he may be too late. She may already be on a ferry headed toward Gaia.

He hurries down the hallway, ignoring the startled exclamations of the maids. He doesn't have time to stop and talk—he needs to get to her chambers! He needs to catch her before she leaves, to ask her if everything is fine—to ask her if *they* are fine.

He skids to a stop in front of her door, smoothing his hands down his wrinkled shirt. He would have changed out of his outfit from last night and made himself presentable, but he was in too much of a hurry. When he's running his fingers through his hair, he notices that her door is cracked open.

He frowns, a crease forming between his brows. He rests his palm against the door, debating if he should open it.

Sunlight seeps across the floor and through the crack of the door. He pushes it open hesitantly, not wanting to walk in on her. But she wouldn't leave her door open if she's here, would she? But would she leave it open while she's gone?

Confused, he steps into the chilly room. The window beside the bookshelf is letting light in, highlighting the dust motes floating in the air. Her bed is perfectly made, and her wardrobe is closed. It looks like no one was even here. Not for weeks, maybe. She must not have spent a lot of time situating her possessions, really making these chambers her own.

He bites his cheek, glancing around. She must have left in quite a hurry this morning if she didn't even bother to shut her door all the way.

He kicks himself, knowing he shouldn't have intruded. This isn't his chambers, and whatever conclusion Ayne came to isn't any of his business. He turns to leave when a sheet of parchment catches his attention. It's poking out from a book on the shelf, just enough to stand out. He presses his lips into a line and tentatively moves toward the bookshelf, the wood floorboards creak beneath him. He plucks the piece of parchment from the book, not knowing what it could be. Did one of his ancestors leave it behind? If he recalls correctly, this room once belonged to Estanova Macellen, the first princess. Or did Ayne put it here? Honestly, it could be any number of people who have had access to this room over the years.

He unfolds the parchment, curiosity driving his actions. He begins to read, his expression contorting from curiosity to embarrassment, then shame.

My dearest,

Read this when you don't want to be alone. Read this when you want to remember me and our brief time together. You'll always have a spot in my heart, Ayne. You were the first girl I ever liked, and I'm glad our parents paired us together—and saw a future between us. And...thank you for saving me. I don't want to recall the time I spent away from home. I can't—not yet. But maybe one day I'll tell you about it. Just know that I'll be in Gaia, waiting for you to return from your journey to Zhongguo.

You are the change this world needs to see right now, Ayne.

-Your loyal subject, Tavo.

Talin folds the parchment back up and returns it

to the book, knowing he shouldn't have continued reading after the letter mentioned Ayne. This is a letter meant *just* for her eyes, and he violated that privacy. But it also reads more like a love letter... Written by the boy, if Talin recalls correctly, that they freed during a court hearing months ago. *Tavo*. A noble's son, and a boy who was courting Ayne.

He can't help but wonder...did Ayne run off to Gaia this morning to see him?

Jealousy rears its ugly little head, and he blanches, knowing he shouldn't be thinking such things. Not of Ayne. She wouldn't go back to her kingdom to meet up with a boy, right after Talin told her he loves her. That would be the biggest stab in the back. She wouldn't do that... Would she?

He gnaws on his bottom lip, ashamed and confused, questioning everything. But he still needs to see her. He wonders if she's boarding a ferry right now. Maybe, if he runs down to the port, he can catch her.

He heads toward the front doors of the palace, hoping he's not too late and he can still catch Ayne.

Unable to find Ayne, he returns to his room to tend to Starlight's wing.

A few days ago, he found an old recipe book in

the kitchen about making salves for injuries from local herbs, so he gathered a few from the back garden and mashed them into a paste to apply to her wing. If it can help battle-worn warriors, then hopefully it can help an injured owl. He doesn't know for sure—but he has to *try*.

Starlight fidgets, trying to back away from the green goop clumped on Talin's fingers. He sighs, reaching toward her. She glares at him with wide, yellow eyes, demanding to know what he's up to and what he has on his hand.

As if the owl can understand him, he tries to explain, "It's a salve. For your wing. It's supposed to mend stuff... You know what mend means, right? Fix? Heal?" He wants to slap himself in the face. Of *course* an OWL doesn't know what the word 'mend' means. The owl can't even speak the Common tongue, for Scota's sake. "Just stay still, please. I want to help you." Starlight stops moving toward the farthest side of the windowsill, just long enough for him to smear a bit of the salve on her injured wing. He doesn't know if she stopped backing up because she trusts him, or if she decided that she might as well keep her energy since it's not like she can go anywhere anyway. Either way, he's taking this as a victory, and hopefully, the salve will help.

"That's a good girl," Talin declares, extending his hand to caress her feathers. "I'll go find you something filling. If you're going to heal quickly, you're going to need your energy." She stares up at him, her yellow eyes twinkling. With a content smile, he leaves her to her spot on the windowsill and grabs a cloak from his wardrobe, clasping it around his shoulders.

On a mission to find her something to eat, Talin hurries from his room, locking the door behind him. He's been emptying the mice traps from the kitchen for the past couple of weeks. He wonders if they've caught anything.

He passes the dining hall on his way down to the kitchen and stops in his tracks when he hears his name. He peers around the doorframe, narrowing his eyes at the table where the entirety of his court is situated. Cedric is standing, his hands splayed out in front of him. The rest of Talin's court is staring up at

Cedric, lips pressed into grave lines.

"Are we sure Prince Talin can rule us—at *fifteen*?" one of the nobles inquires, scoffing. Talin has always known his age would play a factor in every aspect of his life; he's too young to fall in love, but hasn't he? He's too young to be king...but he will be. It's a never-ending cycle of his age determining his capability.

Cedric smacks his palm down on the table. "Haven't we already discussed this? It's too late to change your mind. Queen—*er*—Stella is dethroned. Prince Talin will be king come his birthday. Don't forget how many great rulers were thrust upon the throne at the same age—a few were even younger!"

"But do *you* think he's capable of ruling Klymora? The amount of trafficking and slavery is only increasing. How can a fifteen-year-old boy stop that?" the same noble inquires. Murmurs of agreement rise from among Talin's court. They exchange nervous looks, pondering the future of their country.

Cedric pinches the bridge of his nose. "Prince Talin is going to be king. And, if he's anything like his father, he will lead Klymora into a new, prosperous era. We have all watched Prince Talin grow up. We all knew his father. Think of the resemblance between the two. He carries his father's blood, which means he carries the future of Klymora with him." Cedric sits down and flips open a book. It's small with green leather binding. "Now, we have a coronation to plan. Let's jot down some suggestions and run them by Prince Talin tomorrow."

Talin slips out of view before any of them notice him. He doesn't know exactly what to think. Cedric, who seemed to be against him all this time, is standing up for him to the court? He furrows his brow and runs a hand through his hair, leaving little curls flopped against his forehead.

At least someone doesn't think his young age will be a hindrance.

He continues his walk down to the kitchen, waving to the maids he passes, and greeting the cooks who slip out of the doors to grab something from storage.

"What brings you down here at this time of day, *King* Talin?" Jacque asks, smiling at the boy. He swipes his finger along the side of a knife, dropping the remnants of the herbs he's chopping onto a cutting block.

Talin slinks around the center worktable to search the perimeter of the kitchen. "I was hoping I could help you clear out some of those mouse traps."

The cook raises an eyebrow, setting his knife aside and clapping the herbs from his hands. "Mouse traps? What do you need with dead mice?"

Talin stoops down to look under the metal shelf that holds all the pots and pans. He catches sight of a little skinny tail trailing from a trap. He reaches over and lifts the trap, grabbing only the little wooden piece near the top—farthest from the dead rodent as possible. When he stands up with the trap, the cook gives a little squeak of surprise and mild protest.

The mouse is brown with a white stomach, its whiskers sprouting from a cute, pointed face. Its beady black eyes are slightly open.

The mouse looks so small and innocent that it makes Talin's heart hurt. He doesn't like coming down here and seeing the dead rodents, but Starlight needs food, and he certainly doesn't want to go scavenge in the garden and kill something on his own. This mouse is already dead, so becoming a meal for Starlight is a better fate than being tossed in the trash.

Talin gives the cook a nod before heading out of the kitchen, carrying his prize through the hallways up to his room. He knows the cook must think he's strange or up to something macabre, but Starlight needs to eat. It may be best to not draw more attention to her than he already has. Not everyone likes animals.

He slips back into his room and releases a sigh of relief. He doesn't want to run into someone and start talking about the future, his coronation, or *anything*. Today, he just wants to look after Starlight and forget about the rest of the world.

He sets the mouse trap on the floor and squats, freeing the dead mouse. He moves the trap so the mouse lies on the floor, and then he approaches the windowsill, where Starlight is fast asleep. He frowns, he feels bad about messing with her sleeping schedule, but he's not nocturnal, so unless he decides to break into the kitchen in the middle of the night and steal the dead mice from the mouse traps, this is the best he can do.

He gently nudges Starlight until her eyes snap open and she glares at him.

"I brought you some more food," Talin declares, sweeping his hand toward the mouse lying statue still on the floor.

Starlight, as if she understands him, follows his line of sight, squinting skeptically at the mouse. Her eyes flick back to him as if to accuse him: *you brought me another dead mouse? Am I not good enough for fresh food?*

"Here, let me help you over there," Talin says, lifting her gently into his arms and setting her down on the floor beside the mouse.

At first, Starlight just blinks at the mouse, unsure if she should eat it. But after Talin nudges her forward, she takes the mouse into her beak and begins to devour it, as if she hasn't eaten in days.

He sits down and crosses his legs, watching Starlight and trying to figure out a plan to keep her fed and healthy until he can release her back to the wild where she belongs.

Ayne would have an idea. She usually does.

CHAPTER TWENTY-ONE

Her Future

T alin can feel her arrival before he even sees her—like a disruption in the air or like the sun is suddenly ultra-bright. He sits up from the windowsill where he is stroking Starlight's feathers and jumps when there's a knock at the door. His heart is beating fast, but he can't tell if it's from being nervous that it might be Ayne—the girl he loves—or that it could be someone bringing grave news. His tongue flicks across his dry lips as he stares at the door, contemplating.

With hope, he crosses over to the door and cracks it open, peering into the hallway to identify the knocker. When his eyes meet a pair with golden flecks, his heart bursts in his chest, and he throws the door open, pulling her into a hasty embrace.

"Ayne! You're back," Talin exclaims, crushing her with the strength of his hug.

Ayne taps his arm until he releases her, then chuckles while smoothing the sparkly purple dress she's wearing. "I just had to discuss something with my parents and my sister. I told you I would be back, silly." She looks around him and into the room, pursing her lips at the sight of Starlight's condition. "You must be starving the poor thing." She pushes past him and kneels beside the windowsill, leveling her face with Starlight's, who is sound asleep now that the sun is up again. "What has she been eating?"

"That's what I wanted to talk to you about. There are only so many dead mice I can smuggle from the kitchen before people become suspicious," Talin declares, offering Ayne a sheepish smile when she raises an eyebrow at the mention of the soon-to-be king smuggling dead rodents from around the palace.

Ayne bites her lip and shakes her head gingerly. "That won't do. She needs to hunt." Something shivers under her long black hair that flows over her shoulders and she chuckles, nuzzling it with her cheek. "Not you, Caz. Don't worry. After last time, I don't think Starlight here is going to try to eat you again. Besides...you're an immortal, why are you afraid?" Caz doesn't answer, he just continues to shiver, making Ayne's hair bounce slightly since Caz isn't currently visible to the human eye.

"Any suggestions?" Talin asks, stepping toward Ayne, who is intently studying the sleeping owl. "I need her to heal quickly so I can return her to the wild and not disrupt her life any more than I already have."

Ayne shoots him a meaningful look. "Well, maybe she shouldn't try to eat my pet." She shrugs one shoulder—the one that Caz isn't nesting on— and sighs. "But you're right. She needs a constant stream of mice—or small creatures she can hunt— while being protected inside the palace and not left out with other wild animals. Do you know a place that fits those requirements?" She lifts an eyebrow, turning her quizzical expression to him.

Talin gets momentarily distracted by how the

160

golden sun turns Ayne's raven-feather hair almost brown, and how it speckles across her tan skin and makes her eyes sparkle. Then he remembers where they're at and that he's supposed to come up with a literate response. "Um...I don't know..." He chews on his lip, trying to give this serious matter more thought. Where in the palace is a spot constantly trodden by small prey? Well, it would have to be somewhere the maids don't go since they keep everything ship-shape. A torchlight flickers in his mind, and he grins. Ayne hops to her feet.

"You have an idea?" she says enthusiastically, rocking back and forth on her feet.

"I think I just might." Talin turns on his heel and practically runs toward the door before slamming to a stop and almost toppling over. Dread settles upon his shoulders. "No. I don't think that will work, after all."

Ayne crosses her arms. "Why? What is it?"

He turns around and frowns, his posture sagging. "The dungeon."

Ayne nods. "There would be mice and other creepy crawlies. That could be the perfect spot—"

"Except..." Talin drawls.

"Except?" Ayne tilts her head.

Talin nods. "Except it also has my mother, for the time being."

Talin slips the key into the lock of the dungeon and twists, sighing as he tugs open the heavy door. The guard stationed at the door jumps up from the stool he's resting on and stands alert, bowing to Talin. Before the guard can say anything, Talin gestures to the farthest cell in the palace dungeon, the same one that Faramund was locked in not long ago. The guard gets the message and heads up the short flight of stairs, giving the future king privacy with his convicted mother.

Talin purses his lips, straightening his posture and tilting his chin up. He's not here for his mother. He couldn't care less about visiting her, about hearing any of the excuses she would surely come up with. He's here to find Starlight a safe place where she can catch mice and heal. As long as she stays away from his mother, no one should hurt her —and he doubts even his mother would. Owls are

162

sacred, beautiful creatures. Even a monster like his mother knows that.

Starlight is bundled in Ayne's arms, barely conscious, with one eye slightly parted. "Where should she go?" Ayne whispers, trying not to alert Stella of their presence.

Talin glances around the dreary dungeon—it's barely more than a short hallway with a few cells, but there's a small nook at the base of the stairs that's concealed in shadow. There are a few barrels in the corner, reeking with foul liquid, and an old bench. He kneels, dirtying his trousers on the floor, and peers under the bench. It's rather deep and would be the perfect spot for her to bundle up. It's enclosed in shadows and on the same route a mouse would take when navigating the dungeon.

Talin glances up at Ayne and gestures to the bench. "This might work. I don't think we'll be able to find a better spot."

Ayne purses her lips, but kneels and tilts her head, considering. Her grip tightens a fraction on Starlight as if she doesn't want to let the owl go. Then, with a sigh, she holds the bundle out to Talin, her bottom lip puckering slightly.

"She will be fine," Talin whispers, a smile

tugging at the corners of his lips. "Really, Ayne. This is the best we can do...don't you think? I'll bring Starlight down here every day to hunt." He looks down at the beautiful feathered face of the owl sleeping in his arms, knowing he said all that to comfort not only Ayne—but also himself. She will be fine, won't she? Starlight isn't so injured that she can't hunt for herself, right?

Ayne rests her hand on his shoulder gently and gives him a tiny nod.

He sets Starlight under the bench, and she blinks, her yellow eyes training on him. He nods to her reassuringly. He knows this will be the best thing for her. Animals get hurt all the time in the wild— and they can take care of themselves. Starlight will be fine. He will make sure she is.

Talin gives her one last stroke before pushing himself to his feet and sharing a knowing, concerned look with Ayne.

Then he leans against the opposite wall to give her space to hunt.

CHAPTER TWENTY-TWO

His Birthday

The wind howls outside, carrying flurries of gentle snowflakes toward the white-blanketed village of Caledonia. It always seems to snow on his birthday, which he loves. It's almost tradition to look out the window and watch the snowflakes fall, to try and make out the intricate one-of-a-kind designs.

The smell of warm bread and melted cheese carries on the cold draft slipping underneath the kitchen door and from the cracked corners of the windowsill. He lets his eyes linger on the snow for a moment longer before turning around, a smile already plastered across his face.

"So, this is what you were up to," Talin exclaims, crossing his arms and giving her a conspiratorial look. Ayne grins sheepishly, lifting the tray of goodies.

"It's your birthday, Talin, and since you were busy with meetings all day, I thought we could do something tonight." She sets the tray on the worktable and wanders into the hallway, giving Talin a moment to examine the food tray closer.

There's a plate of fresh sliced bread, some with melted herbs and cheese, a teapot steaming with jasmine tea, and another plate filled with round crackers and pieces of bleu cheese. He chuckles, remembering back to their first night when he prepared her almost the exact meal in the exact place. It seems so long ago, though it wasn't really.

He feels as if he and Ayne have been friends forever. As if they've grown up together, always being there for one another. He can't imagine his life without her—no matter if he remains just a friend or becomes something more. He'll just be happy to be there for her, no matter what.

Ayne slips back into the kitchen and closes the door quietly, making sure that the rest of the palace remains asleep. Surely, they're breaking some rule of etiquette—not like they've followed many to begin with.

Ayne has a blanket she snatched from her chambers bundled in her arms. With a grand flourish, she spreads it across the floor and cocks her head, laughing. "Much better than a burlap sack with rice grains everywhere, wouldn't you say?"

Talin nods in agreement. The burlap sack was a last-minute decision since Ayne is a princess—and once upon a time, was a very proper one at that—he couldn't just invite her to sit on the bare floor.

She grabs the tray and sets it down on the center of the blanket, spreading the simple skirt of the light blue dress she's wearing around her. She blinks up at him, the corners of her eyes crinkling with satisfaction. "Happy birthday, Talin. You're fifteen now!"

He beams, sitting down next to her and crossing his legs. "And in a few short months, you will be fourteen."

She waves his comment away. "Today isn't about me. Now, let's eat before the bread gets cold."

He rubs his palms together and feverishly digs in, the fragrant bread toys with his senses. He can't help the little glob of drool that escapes the corner of his mouth, earning a light-hearted smack from Ayne, who's trying so very hard not to burst into laughter.

Between mouthfuls of cheesy bread and crackers, Ayne asks, "So, what was your birthday wish?"

Talin finishes off another piece of bread—the herb ones without the cheese, since he stays away from the stuff—and wipes his hands on his trousers, throwing decorum to the wind. When he glances around, taking in the night lit by the moon reflecting off the ever-thickening blanket of snow outside, and his beautiful Ayne sitting across from him, a crumb balancing on her upper lip, he realizes what he truly wants for his birthday.

"This." His answer is simple, but it's true. Nothing could make him happier.

CHAPTER TWENTY-THREE

His Coronation

T alin stares at himself in the long mirror that is situated in the corner of the dining hall. Cedric, who took the reins on organizing his entire coronation, deemed this section as his preparation space—since all he has to do is walk out the dining hall doors and down the hall to thunderous applause, then step out into the back gardens, where the entire population of Caledonia—as well as some noble guests visiting from other cities—will be waiting.

169

As the Father of Caledonia's Church, Father Brown, mutters blessings from Scota, he will lower the very same crown that used to be Talin's father's onto Talin's head. And then he will be king. At fifteen. Barely, since his birthday, and that dream-like night he spent snacking on the kitchen floor with Ayne, was yesterday.

He smooths his hand down the baby blue suit he's wearing; the collar is ruffled, and the tail is forked. The cufflinks he's wearing were retrieved from his father's personal stash. Miss Dendlewind told him that they're supposedly the very same ones that King Archibald—his father—wore on the day of *his* coronation.

His heart thumps in his chest, and he suddenly feels hot, as if he's melting. He tugs on the collar of his suit, trying to take deep breaths. What is happening to him? Is he going to have a heart attack and die right before becoming king? How would that look? Who would rule and lead his people then?

A few maids flitter about the room, dusting this and that and finalizing some last-minute details with Cedric, who's lurking near the doors, giving Talin an odd look.

Talin gulps, fanning himself. Maybe the cool air

will help him feel better. Maybe he should step outside and take a deep breath, enjoy the sight of the snow-laden ground. Maybe he should find Ayne. She always seems to make him feel better.

Talin looks around for a chair, needing to sit down and clear his head.

He catches the attention of a maid and asks for a chair—practically begs, since he's so distraught. She quickly drags one over from the table, the legs squeaking against the polished wood floor the entire way.

When Talin collapses into the chair, staring at himself in the long mirror and trying to wrap his head around his entire life shifting, Cedric makes his way toward him, appearing concerned.

Cedric snaps his fingers and whispers something into the ear of a passing maid, who nods and hurries from the dining hall. Talin has no clue what he said —maybe Cedric was saying that Talin isn't fit to be king and shouldn't go through with the coronation!

Cedric kneels in front of Talin and tilts his head, trying to read the creases of Talin's brow and the beads of sweat sliding down his cheek, even though it's quite chilly.

"Prince Talin," Cedric starts, taking the glass of

water from the maid when she hurries back. He hands it to Talin and gestures for him to drink it. Talin does so immediately, needing the chill to tame the burning he's feeling and soothe his constricting throat. "I think I know what's wrong."

Talin sits up, taking another long swig of the water, desperate yet hesitant to know Cedric's diagnosis. "You do?"

Cedric nods. "You're having a panic attack. They're really normal. Even I get them."

"They are? I'm not *dying*?" Talin can feel himself start to calm a bit, knowing that he's not going through this alone—and that he will make it out of this. "Why does this happen?"

Cedric pats Talin's knee softly, offering him a sympathetic smile. "You're growing up. You're realizing there's more to life than playing games. You're worried about things—which means you care. Just take a few deep breaths and think about something—or someone—that makes you happy. It will get better if you can calm your mind."

Talin takes a deep breath in, filling his lungs with the sharp, chilly air, then releases it in a quick puff. He does it again and again, switching his thoughts to Ayne. Of their time under their tree. Of their nighttime meals in the kitchen. Of planning and plotting all the ordeals in his life with her. Of mending Starlight and the countless trips they took down to the dungeon to let her hunt. And of that very first dance they shared when he realized that beneath the princess—there's just *Ayne*. A kind soul with a big heart. And the mouse-like creature with the fluffy tail that sits perched on her shoulder.

His heartbeat starts to slow, and the chilly temperature begins to kiss his damp neck. He sighs, takes the last sip of the water, and smiles at Cedric, who's still studying him. "Thank you, Lord Hemmingway."

Cedric lets out a sigh of relief before pushing back to his feet, then nods, as if saving Talin's life from this "panic attack" was no big deal. "Of course, Prince Talin." A chorus of applause rises from the awaiting crowd in the garden. Cedric gives Talin's outfit a once-over, plucking a piece of lint from his shoulder and straightening his ruffled collar, before announcing, "It's time."

Talin stands up from the chair, feeling better about today than he has since his mother was arrested. He presses the pad of his thumb to the silver cufflink engraved with Klymora's national symbol—the owl—knowing that his father is standing alongside him in spirit, and he will never have to serve this kingdom alone.

He's going to follow in the footsteps of the greatest king Klymora has ever known.

His father.

The gardens don't look like the gardens anymore. They're layered in snow with even more falling from the sky, and the entire length in front of the palace is packed with chairs. Potted bushes in the shape of mirrors, keys, and stacks of books, line the sides of the sitting area, enclosing them from the rest of the sprawling gardens.

He steps out of the doors to find the eyes of hundreds of people firmly plastered on him. Cheers erupt, making his chest constrict with that horrible "panic attack" feeling again, and he desperately searches for any familiar faces in the massive crowd.

He catches sight of Lord and Lady Hart in the second row. They're grinning and mouthing how proud they are. He finds Miss Dendlewind with a little blonde boy beside her. Her eyes are red from crying, and the little boy seems amped by all the excitement. Then his eyes land on a head of black hair streaked through with gold and silver strands and the most magnificent sun-kissed skin. Ayne is wearing a two-skirted purple dress covered in tiny, sparkling stones. They sweep up from the hem of her skirt and twist around toward her midsection before disappearing. It reminds him of snow catching on the wind. Maybe that's why she chose it.

The pride in Ayne's eyes is enough to make him start tearing up. He can't cry now—not when he has to stand in front of his people. Not when this moment marks the day he becomes King of Klymora. The day his entire life officially changes.

He steadies himself and turns toward the dais, mounting the step to the silver throne and taking a seat. From this spot, as he looks out at the smiling faces of his people, he realizes how blessed he is. How determined and thankful he is that he gets the chance to rule, to lead these people into a prosperous era.

Father Brown lifts the silver chalice from the

pedestal situated to the left of the throne and crosses to Talin, standing beside him just enough that the majority of the crowd can still see him.

Father Brown's intricate robes are pure white with beading along the stole depicting the goddess, Scota, as she looks upon the world of her creation.

Father Brown's gravelly voice is surprisingly loud, reaching the ears of every onlooker. "Do you, Prince Talin Macellen of Klymora, swear to uphold the legacy of this great kingdom and do right by everyone who lands on her shores?"

Talin's tongue feels heavy. "I do."

"And do you swear to try your hardest, every day that you shall rule, to help this great kingdom overcome turbulence, opposition, and conflict so that all your subjects shall have prosperous, content lives?"

Talin looks out over the crowd that's hanging on the Father Brown's every word. "I do."

"Finally, do you, Prince Talin Macellen, son of the late king and queen Archibald and Stella Macellen, swear to put this kingdom and all who inhabit her first and foremost?"

Talin lifts his chin. "I do."

Father Brown nods once, then brings the chalice

to Talin's lips, letting the sweet, red substance slide down his throat. "Then I, with the gift of Scota above me, hereby declare you King Talin Macellen of Klymora. May you take this great kingdom into another era."

The crowd erupts, jumping to their feet and hollering at the top of their lungs. Flowers fly from the crowd and scatter around his feet. It's so loud that his ears start to hurt—but he wouldn't change this for anything.

He wants to rule his people—to better their lives —more than anything else.

He glances up at the clouds, knowing his father is with him. His thumb rubs the indent of the owl on his cufflink.

When he meets Ayne's eyes again in the crowd, he tears up. But this time, he doesn't try to push them away. He lets them fall down his cheeks and mingle with the flower petals coating the dais.

CHAPTER TWENTY-FOUR

The Elm

T alin peers up at the sky, snowflakes flitting down between the branches of the elm tree and freckling his cheeks. He lays down and rests his hands on his stomach, ignoring the bite of the cold ground. Most of the ground beneath the tree is relatively dry—considering the branches keep a lot of the snow away.

Ayne lays down beside him.

For a moment, they're both silent, processing the entire afternoon.

He's king. Officially king.

"What now?" Talin asks, knowing he should probably be the one to come up with an answer since it's his responsibility as the leader. But he likes to hear what Ayne thinks.

Ayne moves her hand toward his, clasping them together. She provides him with a little warmth. "I've been meaning to talk to you about that. The evening of the Autumn Ball, when I hurried back to Gaia, I said I had just realized something. And now I'm ready to tell you."

Talin faces her, watching the soft bow of her lips move as she takes a sharp breath of air.

"I've always wanted to...make a change. Help people. And I realized...that Gaia doesn't need me. Not really. They need a queen who can rule them. Who knows what they want and what they need. I would do an excellent job, *clearly*, but Gaia doesn't need me to inspire change." She faces him, her thick, black eyelashes clumping together with falling snowflakes. "I want to stay here. I want to rule the court. I want to help you free people. I think...I'm needed *here*. That this is the place I'm meant to be." She takes a deep breath and tilts her head slightly, staring up at the falling snowflakes and the gray sky.

179

"I think this must be what she meant..."

"Who?" Talin asks, his mind reeling as he tries to process what Ayne's declaring.

"Estanova. Your ancestor. The day I left for Zhongguo, she told me that there's a third prophecy. *'Soon, when the three warring countries unite—then there will be a sacrifice.'* I think she meant me. I want to sacrifice my crown, as Klymora, Gaia, and Zhongguo unite." She bites her bottom lip and winces. "What do you think? Is that...okay?"

He doesn't know how he feels about his ancestor's ghost floating around reciting prophesies... Is she here now? His eyes quickly flit around, wondering if he can see her.

Talin digests her confession. Ayne wants to stay...*here*? With him? She wants to rule his court? He nods. "Welcome, Princess Ayne Edelweiss, leader of my court."

She smiles, turning to peer up at the barren branches again. "It looks like someone came to visit us."

Talin follows her gaze up to a pair of yellow eyes staring down at them. Starlight tilts her head, watching the two under the elm tree. "Hi, beautiful creature. Did you come to congratulate me?"

Starlight seems to laugh at him, flapping her wings before tucking them close to her body, and turning her attention to the desert land across the Abhainn River.

Talin takes another calming breath, knowing he probably won't get many chances in the coming months. But right now, he just wants to live in this moment, under this snow-speckled sky, beside the girl he loves.

Tomorrow he will focus on being king.

End of Book 3

Continue the adventure in book 4, *The King's Sorcerer*.

If you enjoyed *The Prince of Klymora*, please leave a
review with your thoughts!
<u>Goodreads</u>
<u>Amazon</u>
We're looking forward to seeing you on our next
adventure!

Acknowledgments

Thank you to everyone who has made it this far into Ayne and Talin's journey, and to the community of authors I've connected with through Instagram who constantly hype up my books. I would like to give a special shout-out to Tuesday Simon (@tuesday.simon.author) and Jacie Neher (@jacieneher), two exceptional, encouraging authors I've met through Instagram.

I'd like to give a massive thank you to Nonni. Without you, I wouldn't be a published author. Thank you for reading all my stories. Your critiques are invaluable.

Thank you, Mom. You're my biggest inspiration. I cannot wait until we have a library dedicated just to our books.

Thank you, Sydney, for being more supportive of my writing than you have been in the past (lol, love you, sister.)

I would also like to thank Jacob for proofreading and critiquing my work, and for surprising me two and a half years ago when you bought and read my first book without telling me. That was quite a wonderful surprise (though, admittedly, very nerve-wracking.)

And thank you to Papa and Doug, who don't have much to do with my writing, but still are encouraging, nonetheless.

About the Author

Daphne Paige has always loved writing; watching and learning from her mother, who's also a writer. With the majority of her time spent writing, the breaks between stories makes her remember she has an actual life away from her characters.

During those breaks, she loves to play video games, hangout with her various pets, and watch classic black and white films with her family.

Daphne lives in Oregon helping her family with their popcorn business.

Signed books: https://popcorn-publishing.com

Connect with the author on social media:
Instagram: @daphne.paige.books
TikTok: @daphne.paige.books

More by the Author

Kingdoms and Curses:
The Heiress of Gaia
The Empire's Witch
The Prince of Klymora
The King's Sorcerer
(Book 5 Coming Soon…)

Emilia of the Solstice Realm:
Return of Eve
Banished by Darkness
(Book 3 Coming Soon…)

More:
Jess
Forest of Monsters Novella (Coming Soon…)

www.ingramcontent.com/pod-product-compliance
Lightning Source LLC
Chambersburg PA
CBHW022103170626
46808CB00002B/575